Hillel's Glory

B. Heather Mantler

ISBN:978-1-927507-56-8

For he who asked and then waited.

HILLEL SEES OBSTACLES TO HIS GRAND SCHEMES DISAPPEAR AND WELDON IS NOT SURE ABOUT THE FUTURE ANYMORE

Hillel stood out of sight on the balcony as he watched the meddling magician walk out of the courtyard gates. Rana, among others, were down below seeing him off. That was fine, but Hillel had never liked the man being there, so he could not be seen watching the magician leave. People might have wondered and, Hillel did not want that.

Hillel wanted to order the gates to be shut and locked to make sure the magician could not get back in but instead went to the office behind the throne room. He still was not used to calling it his office. His mind kept calling it his father's office, even though it had been his for a full season. As far as everyone knew, his father had disappeared and was never coming back. Those who did know what happened were unwilling to talk about it. Hillel figured it must have been traumatizing if grown fighting men were not willing to speak on the subject. But he was king now, and all that was the past. He had a future to attend to, and with the magician gone, he could do just that.

Hillel closed the door behind him and locked it before sitting down. There was a pile of paperwork from the lower court, but he ignored it. Those peasants did not need his attention, especially since Weldon took care of all the decisions necessary. Hillel never bothered to pay any attention to the papers they kept giving him, so Weldon must take care of those decisions as well.

"Is he gone?" the smooth and deep voice asked from behind Hillel. Hillel did not turn around to look at the being he knew would be more smoke than physical form.

"Left not that long ago," Hillel answered, "He will not bother us and our plans."

"His essence still lingers," the being said, "Are you sure he is gone?"

"I watched him leave," Hillel answered, "I watched the people say good bye. I talked to the castle steward, who assured me the magician's room will be cleaned out before lunch."

"It may just be the amount of power he holds that causes his essence to linger," the being said, "Either way, it will be taken care of. How is our plan coming along?"

"Quite well," Hillel answered, "No one suspects anything. They all see me as a bored and lazy king. I have not accomplished anything since my father's disappearance, and no one expects anything from me."

"Good," the being said, "I sense there are things you should be careful of and people you should watch. They will be the cause of your downfall."

"As long as I have you on my side, there is nothing to stop me from obtaining my goals," Hillel said.

"Be careful your confidence does not bring down the whole plan," the being said. Hillel did not bother to answer because it was gone.

Weldon had not bothered to stand out in the cold wind to bid his goodbyes to the magician, Luce, as he had not bothered to introduce himself at all during the man's time in the castle. He cared nothing for men who used magic and had little use for them, despite Driscoll's love of all things magical. It was better that Luce was leaving Proster and Weldon hoped he did not plan on ever coming back. Rana would be sad for a while as she got over Luce leaving her behind for his grand quests and wanderings, but she would be better for it in the end. Weldon was sure of that.

Going along the corridor toward his officer, Weldon shuffled the notes the castle steward had given him. The courts had been closed for today, but Weldon still had work to do. That was another reason he did not stand out in the biting wind to see Luce off. Running the castle did not stop just because one mouth left. As king, Hillel probably should have been doing many of these tasks, but Weldon had taken them on while Driscoll had been king and had not bothered to relinquish them. It also meant Weldon knew they would get done. Hillel tended to ignore things until they directly affected him, at which point it was twice the amount of work to deal with the problem.

Weldon opened the door to his office. Both his clerks were off today. Yesterday he had thought of demanding they come into work, but both had worked long passed the time they should have been home for most of the week. He placed some of the papers on the desk to his right and took the rest with him to a larger desk at the far end of the room, which was his desk.

The fire had not been built in the fireplace, and Weldon had told the castle steward not to bother about it. It might have been the early part of spring, but it was usually warm enough in his office for the ink not to freeze. However, for some reason, today the cold bothered Weldon. As he started his paperwork, he thought about making up the fire himself or finding a blanket to wrap around himself. If it were not for the fact that his fingers were not cold, Weldon would have done one or the other. His fingers were always the first things to get cold and the sign he used to know when to warm up, but this was an unnatural cold which would chill the rest of him and left his fingers warm.

Weldon stopped working for several minutes as he thought this over. There had been several other things over the last few months, which bothered him in the same way. The way the barrels of wine had been draining much faster than the cook could explain, the screams coming from the empty dungeon at night, and the disappearance of a couple of dogs who usually hung around the courtyard. The castle steward had reported all of these things to Weldon, but neither could understand what they could all mean.

Picking up his pen, Weldon pushed his thoughts to one side of his mind. He had plenty of paperwork to finish before he could take any serious time to examine all of those reports. He shivered a little as he continued his work, but his fingers were not cold. A knock came at the door.

"Come in," Weldon called without looking up. He was expecting the castle steward to bring him the rest of the inventory for the week and the guard schedules. The door opened, and instead, Rana stepped inside. She wore the deep blue dress today, which was the one she looked best wearing. Likely she wore it to look good for Luce when he looked back that final time before leaving the gate. Weldon expected Rana to be sad, but instead, she seemed worried.

Rana sat down in the chair in front of Weldon's desk with her hands in her lap and a slightly nervous smile on her lips. She was trying not to clasp her hands or twist her fingers.

"Good morning," Weldon said with a smile, "To what do I have the privilege of your company today?"

"I have decided to move out to the country estate," Rana answered.

"But Driscoll requested that you stay and help with advising his son," Weldon said, "I know you and Luce were close and his leaving hurt you, but there are others here who need you."

"I have thought it through," Rana said, "Hillel will never listen to me, no matter how much King Driscoll wanted him to, and most of the other duties I was doing for King Driscoll have disappeared along with him. There is very little for me to do in the city right now. Should that change, I can move back, but I think right now the country estate is the best place for me to be."

"Are you sure?" Weldon asked.

"I am," Rana answered.

"The country estate needs work before anyone can live there," Weldon said.

"It will give me something to do while I find something to occupy my time," Rana said, "I will take my maid and see if I can hire some help from the nearby village. There is a couple who are currently taking care of the place. I will send them a message to let them know I am coming so they can prepare some rooms. Then all I have to do is pack my stuff and be off."

"I would suggest taking a couple of guardsmen with you, at least until you are sure about the people from the village you are hiring," Weldon said, "For your safety."

"Most of them are likely to be busy here," Rana said, "And I would not want to take them away from their duties."

"I will talk to Kapena about it," Weldon said, "Even if there are no guards he can loan out, he will know good ones to hire."

"Okay," Rana said, "I was very much hoping to leave tomorrow morning."

"I will make sure the guards are ready when you are," Weldon said.

"I am going to miss you and Daniella," Rana said, "But this is better for me."

"It is not so far that letters are difficult to send either way," Weldon said, "And if you feel it is right for you then it most likely is, no matter my feelings on the subject. I would suggest you visit Daniella and tell her you are leaving rather than have her find out after you have left."

"I will talk to her sometime this afternoon," Rana

said, "But first, I need to make sure I have everything ready."

"Very well," Weldon said.

"Thank you for being understanding," Rana said.

"As long as you are sure this is right," Weldon said.

"I am," Rana said before she got to her feet. She left Weldon's office.

Weldon looked down at the work he had been doing before Rana came in, but it hardly seemed important now. He had to help his sister prepare for her journey. As much as he did not want her to go, Weldon knew she was set on it, and it was better just to make sure she was ready for it. He left the paperwork on his desk and headed to talk to the captain of the guard as well as the castle steward.

Hillel was on his way to the courtyard to practice with his sword when he heard the voices of Weldon and the castle steward. He stopped while still out of sight and listened.

"I talked to Kapena about it," Weldon said, "He suggested Duard and Havard. I accepted the offer, but Rana should be warned that both only have a month left in their service. I am not sure what else she needed for the journey."

"She asked for food and another trunk," the castle steward replied, "I have talked to the cook, and food will be ready. I have Little Rory searching storage areas for a couple of trunks. He should get back to me shortly, and then I can arrange for them to be taken to Rana's rooms. I have also spoken to Carter, so that he may get the carriage ready and maybe start packing up some of the trunks."

"Good idea," Weldon said, "Rana can take my carriage when she goes to visit Daniella Oakley if that visit has been arranged."

"It has," the castle steward said, "Lady Daniella is expecting her late this afternoon."

"Then it sounds like everything is ready for Rana," Weldon said, "Aside from what she has to do herself."

"Is she sure she has to leave?" the castle steward asked, "The Mungle estate is two days from here. If anything happens, she will be too far away to hear about it in time."

"She feels it would be better for her to go," Weldon said, "And as much as I want to argue, I do not think there is any talking her out of it. She also feels useless with Hillel on the throne and would rather be somewhere she had something to do. The Mungle estate needs some work, so she will start there and figure out what else when that is finished."

"Now, I will have to find someone who can do the jobs she had been doing here," the castle steward said, "She has been very helpful to have around."

"I know," Weldon said, "But she does not think so. I just hope she is right about going."

"I hope so too," the castle steward said.

There was no further conversation, only the sounds of two people going in opposite directions. Hillel looked and saw them both gone. He continued toward the courtyard.

Hillel was not sure why the castle steward would be so sad about Lady Rana leaving. As far as Hillel could tell, she was useless, and her presence made it likely the magician might come back. Lady Rana and the magician might have tried to keep their affair quiet, but they had not succeeded. However, if she was leaving then there was no reason for him to come back, which meant Hillel's plan would have no complications from that direction. Hillel smiled to himself. Everything was going well.

Weldon stood out in the freezing wind as he stared out over the city. He was wearing his cloak, but the wind was too lazy to go around him and instead went right through the thick wool. Weldon paid it no attention as he was lost in thought. He was wandering whether Rana could sense the foreboding, which was hovering over the kingdom. The chill, which froze Weldon's heart but not his fingers, had nothing to do with the outside weather or how many fires burning inside. Something was coming, and it was not going to turn out well for the kingdom.

Rana might be leaving before anything happened, but Weldon was not going to abandon his post. He owed Driscoll for everything he had in this life, and the only way he knew how to repay that debt was to defend the throne of Proster from whatever was threatening it, even if that threat was in the form of the current king. It did not matter what happened and what Hillel did, Weldon would use all his power to keep the kingdom from being destroyed or taken over.

Then again, it might be a good thing Rana was leaving. She would not be anywhere near the centre of the conflict, and thus, she would be safe from harm. If she was safe, then Weldon did not need to worry about her. Rana would be hidden from anyone who would wish her ill-health, leaving Weldon just himself to look after, which would be much easier. Now if he could just figure out where the danger was coming from and how to stop it.

The last light of the day touched the world as if to say good night. It made the world appear orange. Weldon glanced down at the courtyard, expecting only to see the guards. Instead, he saw something that caused more worry for him. Sitting beside the gate looking up at him, was a white wolf. Even in the colours of the sunset, the wolf remained white. And even though Weldon could not see its eyes, he could have sworn it was watching him. Weldon wondered if this wolf was some guardian left by Luce, as the guards did not seem to see it as they walked right by it. If it were, it would leave tomorrow with Rana. If Luce left the wolf, Rana would be the person it would be guarding.

The sun was gone, and the sky grew dark. The torches were lit in the courtyard by the guards. Weldon looked back to the place where the white wolf was and found it was gone. He searched the courtyard with his eyes but did not see it. The chill in his heart caused him to shiver and pull his cloak closer around him, despite how useless it was. He looked around again but still did not see it. Uncomfortable now, Weldon headed inside in hopes of finding his bed warm.

Hillel stayed out of sight as everyone else waited for Rana to come down and say goodbye on her way out of the castle. He supposed he could have stood there with them, but he was far more interested in what people would say if he were not in the room than what they would say to his face. And Rana leaving was hardly an event he would be invited to attend.

Weldon was there, along with the castle steward, the

housekeeper, the cook, and Hillel's own Arabella. And in that order going toward the door. Hillel was not sure why Arabella was there. She did not know Rana all that well, as far as he knew. But he supposed she felt obligated to be there.

Footsteps of two people came toward the entrance. Hillel figured it must be Rana and her maid as the swish of a dress suggested it was not any of the servants. The two stopped right about where Hillel figured Weldon was standing.

"I will miss you," Weldon said, "And I am sure Driscoll would not want you to go, but I understand your reasons for leaving."

"I will miss you, too," Rana responded.

It was quiet, aside from some shuffling. This was likely the castle steward, the housekeeper, and the cook bowing to her as if she was someone important in the castle.

"I am sorry you are leaving," Arabella said, "It was an honour to meet and get to know you."

"It is the same for me," Rana said, "And I wish good luck and fortune in your life."

"You will be missed here at the castle," Arabella replied. Hillel was not sure what she meant by that, but women did not always make sense to him.

A moment of rustling clothing followed and then several minutes of quiet before the door was closed. Everyone headed off to their area of the castle. Hillel waited a few minutes before leaving his hiding place so no one would notice him. Then he headed toward his office. With both the magician and Lady Rana out of the way, his plans would flow much smoother.

Weldon had headed for his office after watching his sister leave and expected it to be a busy morning. However, he noticed Arabella following him. She was quiet, and she did not stop him or interrupt him, just followed him. He wondered but decided she might be uncomfortable talking about what was on her mind out in the castle hallway as there was always someone around to overhear.

They reached the door to his office, and he held it open for her. She stepped inside and headed for the chair in front of his desk. Weldon's clerks were busy working on the paperwork from the last time the courts were open as they were closed again today.

"Perhaps, you two should take a break," Weldon told his clerks. They looked up from their paperwork in surprise. Only once they saw his expression did they wipe off their quills and leave their paperwork. He held the door as they left and then locked it behind them. Then Weldon went to his desk and sat down in the chair.

Arabella was paler than usual and lacked her typical liveliness. She sat like a proper queen and showed no outward signs of nervousness, but there was sadness in her eyes.

"I am sorry for taking up your time," Arabella said, "But I fear your office is the only safe place to talk in the castle."

"You are worried about your safety?" Weldon asked. Weldon thought the one person safe from everything would be Arabella because Hillel would do nothing to hurt her. He practically worshipped at her feet.

"Since Driscoll went missing, Hillel has changed," Arabella said, "I thought I knew him, but he has gotten more aggressive. I fear he might be a danger to everyone around him."

"You think he might attack someone in the castle?" Weldon asked.

"No, he is thinking bigger," Arabella answered, "He has been talking about leaving a legacy of glory in battle."

"We are not at war with anyone," Weldon said, "And to start one would not lead to glory, but a revolt from the people."

"I do not know how he is going to accomplish it," Arabella said, "But he is obsessed with the idea of gaining glory in battle. I am scared of what he will do to start a war. Maybe you can stop him, but it will take as much help as you can muster. I asked Hillel if I could go back to my father's estate, but he will not let me go. I even suggested it would be best for the baby."

"He is not going to let you go anywhere now that you have told him," Weldon said, "From what I have seen of him, he desperately wants this child."

"I know he wants this child," Arabella said, "We have been trying to have this child for a while. Up until now, I wanted the child too. Now I do not think I want the child anymore."

"Of course, you want the child," Weldon said, "I will do everything I can to stop Hillel from starting a war."

"Thank you," Arabella said, "Please do not tell him I talked to you."

"I will not say anything about you coming here to talk to me," Weldon said.

"Thank you," Arabella said. She got up and left the office. Weldon did not bother to watch her go. He stared without seeing down at the paperwork strewn across his desk. There was a lot he had to think about. Weldon did not even notice when his clerks came back to work.

Hillel tapped his fingers on the arms of the throne as the lord in charge of the lower court made his report. There were so many more important things Hillel felt he should be doing, but others seemed to feel this façade of caring was necessary. The lower court did not matter to anyone important as far as Hillel was concerned.

There was some activity at the doorway, and then a group of people entered. They stood aside as they waited their turn to be announced. The crest the group was wearing belonged to Grackle. Hillel kept his face bored and pretended to be paying attention to the lord, who was intoning on about the lower court.

The man droned on for another hour before he finally finished, bowed, and got out of the way. A guard stepped up and bowed.

"A diplomat from Grackle is here to address the court," the guard announced.

"I suppose if they must address us," Hillel said.

The man in the most expensive clothing stepped forward and bowed.

"I am Lord Sedgewick," the man said, "At the request of my king, I bring a possible agreement between our kingdoms."

"No agreement between our kingdoms has ever existed," Hillel said, "I doubt there will ever be any such thing."

"I ask only for some of your time to present the

possible agreement," Lord Sedgewick said.

"The next session of court is not until next week," Hillel said.

"At your schedule," Lord Sedgewick replied with a bow.

"We are unlikely to accept such an agreement," Hillel said.

"As long as you are willing to listen," Lord Sedgewick said.

"Briefly," Hillel said.

Lord Sedgewick bowed before moving back to the rest of the group from Grackle.

"Anything else?" Hillel called when none of the guards stepped forward immediately. No one spoke as they looked for the guard who had stepped out after announcing Lord Sedgewick. Hillel scanned the crowd for half a minute.

"Court dismissed," Hillel announced. He stepped down from the dais and strode out of the throne room while everyone bowed when he passed. Hillel went through the hallways to his father's office. Inside he sat down at the desk. There was a new pile of paperwork, which appeared to be connected to the lower court. Hillel pushed the pile off the desk towards the fire but otherwise paid it no attention.

"This works well with our plan," the voice spoke, but Hillel did not turn towards it.

"It does," Hillel said, "They will be wonderful scapegoats and reasons for war."

"Then you need to make the announcement in the next few days," the voice said, "Otherwise, it will not work."

"Of course," Hillel said, "I know what to do. The

people will believe there is plenty of danger and let me do whatever I want after that."

"Your glory is coming," the voice said.

"As expected," Hillel said as he leaned back in his chair and smiled.

There was a knock at the door. Hillel got to his feet and went to the door. He opened it and found the castle steward standing there.

"Yes?" Hillel asked.

"Lunch is served," the castle steward said with a bow.

"Of course," Hillel said. He stepped out of his office and closed the door behind him. The castle steward stepped out of Hillel's way and waited until Hillel walked by him before heading off. Hillel went to the dining room. Everyone else in the castle was already seated, but the food had not been brought out yet. Arabella was in her seat at the head table. Hillel sat down next to her.

Hillel looked at Arabella and she appeared queasy and pale. He reached out to take her hand.

"Are you all right?" Hillel kept his voice low to avoid anyone overhearing him.

"My stomach is slightly upset," Arabella answered, "I probably just need a little food."

"Perhaps you should take this afternoon to rest," Hillel said, "We do not want either of you to be endangered."

"I will have some lunch and then go up to rest," Arabella said. Hillel smiled at her. She returned his smile, but it was hesitated and uncertain. He kissed her hand before having to let go so the servants could set lunch in front of them.

Arabella reacted as if the food on the plate smelled awful, but she ate a couple of bites anyway. Hillel watched her while he ate. She was slow to pick out a bite and slow to chew. Everything she placed in her mouth caused her to gag slightly, however she did swallow it. Then she swallowed it again. Once she had eaten a few bites, Arabella set her fork down.

"I think I will go rest now," Arabella said.

"I hope you feel better after," Hillel said. Arabella nodded before getting to her feet. No one paid much attention as she left the higher table and headed out of the dining room. Only one other head other than Hillel's followed her progress, and that was Weldon. Hillel might have thought Weldon a danger to his marriage, but Weldon had yet to show interest in any woman who had crossed his path. It was concern for the kingdom that caused Weldon to be worried about Arabella.

It would be Weldon who would be Hillel's biggest problem. He would do his best to prevent any trouble from happening. Fortunately, he was busy running the kingdom and did not have a lot of time to investigate what Hillel was doing. Not that Weldon had not found time to sniff around things before, however, Hillel could easily distract and redirect Weldon's attention.

When he finished eating, Hillel left the dining room. He did not bother to check if anyone was paying attention to his exit. After thinking about going back to his office, Hillel decided instead to go out and practice with his sword.

Weldon sat at his desk and stared at the fire. His clerks had decided they needed the heat, otherwise, he would have left it unlit. Not that he was not cold, so much as the fire gave him no warmth. The paperwork in front of him needed his attention, but Weldon's mind was spinning with numerous thoughts. He knew Hillel had plans, however, he was unsure how to figure out what those plans were. Weldon was also concerned about Arabella. He had talked to one of her servants after she had left lunch early and told she was sick. This Weldon was less worried about because he had been told such sickness was normal with pregnancy. Instead, he was concerned about what Hillel might do to her.

Weldon did not think Hillel would physically hurt her, but that did not stop Hillel from any mental games. She had endangered herself by coming to Weldon about her concerns and telling what she knew about Hillel's plans. Weldon did not think Hillel knew about it, but anything is possible with everything else happening in the castle.

There was a knock at the door causing, Weldon to look away from the fire. One of his clerks put down his quill and got up to answer it. The clerk talked to the person without opening the door enough for Weldon to see who it was. He could, however, hear the visitor was female. After a moment, the clerk opened the door, and a lady stepped inside. Weldon did not recognize her as any of the ladies who came to court.

She wore a light pink dress with white lace trim, her blonde hair was wrapped in an intricate design with a pink ribbon woven through it, and her blue eyes were bright. With a pale complexation, she was nobility. Her lips were soft pink and appeared highly kissable. Weldon felt his heart beating faster. He worked carefully to make sure it was not visible that his breath had briefly caught in his throat.

Weldon got to his feet as she approached his desk.

"Can I help you?" Weldon asked.

"I was told that if I brought my letter for Lady Rana to you, you could get it to her," the lady said.

"Of course," Weldon said, "You must be Lady Daniella. Lady Rana has told me a lot about you, and I am sorry we have not met before this."

Lady Daniella's cheeks went slightly pink as her lips curved a bit.

"My father does not encourage me to visit the castle," Daniella said, "Lady Rana did invite me to visit a few times, but I had to turn her down. I am only here because I told my father I was delivering a letter without telling him where."

"I can understand your father's concern about coming to the castle," Weldon said, "But it is quite safe to visit."

"I doubt my father would change his mind on the matter," Daniella said, "Once he has decided something, it is tough to change it. Lady Rana lived in the castle without coming to harm, but my father believes she left because she was in danger."

"It was not danger that caused her to leave," Weldon said, "More she felt useless here because King Hillel does not believe in taking advice from a female. It is hard being an advisor when the person does not listen."

"It is good that there is no danger in visiting the castle," Daniella said, "Because I will be coming to drop off letters for Lady Rana."

"I will gladly make sure they are sent on to her," Weldon said.

"Thank you," Daniella said, "I know she has not

been gone long, but I already miss her."

"I understand," Weldon said, "I appreciated having her around to ask for her advice on matters. There have been many times she saw an option I could not find no matter how long I thought about the matter."

"My father did not think her advice was good," Daniella said, "But she was much better at predicting the outcome of my suitors than he has been, though she never mentions her conclusion when it does happen. She just acts surprised when it does not work out."

"Sounds like Lady Rana," Weldon said with a smile.

"Yes," Daniella smiled back at him, "She is like that."

One of the clerks cleared his throat to get Weldon's attention. Weldon reluctantly took his eyes of Daniella to look at the clerk holding a pile of papers.

"Unfortunately, it seems my work requires my attention," Weldon said, "But I will get the letter to Lady Rana and any others you bring to me." He gave her another smile.

"Thank you," Daniella said with a smile in return. She turned and left the office. Weldon stood still and watched until he could not see her. Only then did he turn his attention to the clerk.

Hillel stopped to catch his breath as his sparring opponent did the same on the opposite side of the practice area. Something caught Hillel's attention, and he turned to look. Sitting on the far side of the courtyard near the wall was a white wolf. Its bright blue eyes stared back at him. No one else in the whole courtyard appeared to have seen it, even though others had looked that direction.

Hillel's attention was moved back to his opponent for a second before he glanced back to the white wolf. It was no longer there, and Hillel looked around for it. The white wolf was gone as if it had never been. Hillel could not spend any more time looking for the creature as his opponent was now charging him. Hillel went back to focusing on the practice fight.

After they finished sparring and cleaning up, Hillel went to his office. He sat down in the chair but ignored the pile of paperwork that had been set on his desk as if someone expected him to do something with it.

"I sense a question," the voice said, "I hope you are not questioning our plan."

"I am not questioning our plans," Hillel said, "I saw a creature in the courtyard, and I wonder what it is."

"What did this creature look like?" Hillel felt some uncertainty coming from the voice.

"It was a white wolf," Hillel answered. There was a quick flash of fear from the being, and then it was covered over.

"The white wolf is no worry to our plans," the voice said.

"What is the white wolf?" Hillel asked.

"It is not of this world," the voice answered, "And it will not cause us issues."

"Very well," Hillel said, "But why was only I am to see it?"

"I told you, it is not of this world," the voice said, "Think about it no more. Our plan is on schedule."

Hillel sat in quiet as he felt the presence go away. He continued to be still for several minutes afterward. It was then that he remembered the book he had seen once on the bookshelf. It had pictures of creatures that were magical in nature. Hillel got up and went to the book shelf. He looked for books with blue covers as he remembered the book having one, but he could not think of the title. He picked the first one off the shelf and opened it to the first page.

Once upon a time there, lived a Prince who lived in a far away kingdom ruled by his father. The Prince was a kind soul, but his father was a cruel man. During the Prince's lifetime, the kingdom had been on no less than six wars. Despite being used to it, the Prince felt wars were not right.

It was the Prince's sixteenth year when the diplomat from the neighbouring kingdom arrived with his daughter. The Prince was smitten with the daughter at his first sight of her but knew his father would kill the diplomat and his family at the first disagreement. The Prince would have to figure out some way to save her.

Hillel put the book back on the shelf and moved on to the next blue book. He opened it to the first page.

The world was hers, all she had to do was reach the gem. Despite all the temptations placed in front of her, she had kept the gem as her goal and ignored everything else. Now the only thing between her and the gem was a long stone staircase. She could taste the power and feel the coolness of the gem on her palm. Smiling, she stepped on to the first stair. The whole cave shook causing, dust to rain down on her. Her smile disappeared, and she froze. As if it had just been an earthquake, the cave shook. It stopped when she didn't move to the next step. She pulled out the scroll and unrolled it. Rereading it carefully, she checked to see if she missed anything.

Hillel put the book back on the shelf and moved on

to the next blue book. He opened it to the first page.

Aldous was glad when the guards finally removed the shackles and pushed him into the small cell. The cell might have been drafty and dark, but at least it was private. Something he had not had since the war between Aldous's kingdom and Casimir's kingdom had begun. Aldous knew that as a prisoner of war, it was expected he would be paraded for the crowds, like any other king taken prisoner. He was just happy the parading was over for the moment, and he did not have to be on display for a while. Casimir might put Aldous on trial for any crimes that counted as going to war in the next week or so. Aldous would handle that with the dignity befitting a king when the time arrived, but, while in this cell, Aldous was happy to be just another prisoner.

Hillel put the book back on the shelf and moved on to the next blue book. He opened it to the first page.

The statement was made, the declaration shouted out and the words echoing. For all the loud voices, there were none cheering. The mesmerizing words of man worthless as they fall from the air. Sentences, words, letters all lay on the cold metal ground, forgotten and lost. To see the world in the oblivion man created, to know the casualties that lie still, to remember the past mistakes that are repeated. Humans are still alive, but they have stolen life from themselves and each other.

No one stands alone, no one is a minority, no one is different. The cycle is just going without any rest; a person is born, joins the line, walks until they collapse and then are laid to rest. The world has become cold and waits only for destruction. Hope stuck in the box and forgotten, love lay only in dreams, and dreams lost in the never ending turmoil people call life.

I tell you this because some day some one will see, some one will know. Words forgotten, pictures forgotten, colours forgotten, books forgotten, television forgotten, computers forgotten.

I have one thing left, people have one thing left, and all but me have been blind to it. Light, glowing, radiant and beautiful. Light for me creates hope, hope brings back dreams, dreams show me love. In this cold, dark world. I alone feel the warmth and see the light. I want to share, but the words echoed unheard in the silence. Hope seems lost at times, but the light is always there.

Hillel put the book back on the shelf and moved on to the next blue book. He opened it to the first page.

Return to the land, the land where you belong. The land that calls to you, that you see every time you dream. That pesters you, tempts you, and doesn't want to let you go. Return to the land.

The ocean, the jungle, the town, the garden, the desert. It contains all of these, or it can contain none of these. It fills you while you're there, the memory warms you, and you are empty until you go back.

Hillel put the book back on the shelf and moved on to the next blue book. He opened it to the first page.

Once upon a time in a small town called Hefton, there lived a tailor. His name was Tate, and his shop was the last building before the road headed into the forest, which surrounded the small town. Tate was a cheery individual who did good work but was not known for his brains. He rarely went out, but when he did, he practically skipped rather than walk. He had stick like arms and legs with a body to match. He had glasses that were always sliding down his nose and seemed like they would slide right off if he did not push them up every minute or so. His clothing fit perfectly, but the hat he wore was floppy and fell on the top of his glasses, making them slide down farther. His shoes were also a size too big and caused many wonder how he managed to skip without falling on his nose. Some of the people in the small town would make fun of him, but he just smiled and continued on his way. His life was happy in his small house.

Hillel put the book back on the shelf and moved on to the next book, to find there were no more of that colour. He looked over the shelf again but could not see any other books with blue covers. Hillel thought about it, but he was sure the book had a blue cover. As much as he might have considered going through every book on the shelf, Hillel decided it was not required and that he did not need to know what the white wolf was if it was not going to cause issues with the plans.

With that thought, Hillel left his study so he could get some work done.

The demon had settled himself near the fireplace in Lord Weldon's office. It had been his favourite place to be of late. He had followed Hillel around until he realized Hillel did little of interest and was faithfully following the plan. Knowing Hillel did not need the supervision, the demon had found himself following Lord Weldon around. This had proved to be a more useful hobby. This pastime was when the demon learned of Lady Rana's leaving and Lady Arabella's concerns over her husband. This was the closest the demon could get to know what is going on with the enemy. When the lord from Grackle arrived, the demon had tried following him around, but that proved to be a waste of time. The lord spent his time gossiping with the nobility, who had nothing to do with running the kingdom. Overall, the lord of Grackle seemed to be ignorant, full of himself, and confused as to how things work.

Now the demon had found something even more useful. Lord Weldon had come under the foolish human emotion of love. Since the young lady had visited him, he had been easily distracted and spent time staring in space. The young woman had not looked so attractive to the demon, but humans usually did not. Lord Weldon has been shivering for the past few days, at least, and now suddenly, he appeared to have warmed up.

Apparently, that would be Lord Weldon's afternoon, as he did little less with the time. The demon might have stayed longer, but he felt he needed to get other things done. He left the love sick Lord Weldon and went out of the castle. The being he was looking for was waiting for him in an alley way outside the castle walls.

"Whats yous wants?" the being asked as the demon settled into a squat.

"Death," the demon answered before offering a piece of fabric.

The being took the fabric and stuffed it into its mouth. After a moment of mulling, it swallowed the material.

"As yous wants," the being said.

"Go," the demon said. The being sniffed the air before disappearing. The demon smiled to itself. There would be no more Lady Rana to come back and attempt to stop the plan. He turned to head back into the castle and found himself faced with the Reese.

"You called me," the Reese said.

"I did," the demon said, "I wish the death of a nobleman of this kingdom."

"You may wish his death all you want," the Reese said, "My bargain is not to work in this kingdom as long as the Proster line reigns."

"Your bargain?" the demon asked, "Why would you put yourself in such a situation to turn down work?"

"Because our weaknesses are our destruction," the Reese answered, "And I let mine make my bargain."

"Perhaps you can keep the White Wolf away," the demon said, "I have heard you know it."

"The price for such a request is more than you can pay," the Reese said, "If you wish to control this kingdom, it is completely up to you to gain it and to overcome the challenges already in your way."

"You will not help me at all?" the demon asked.

"You cannot afford the price for what you ask," the Reese answered.

Before the demon could say anything more, the Reese was gone. The demon looked around, though he knew he would not see anything. The Reese was gone. The demon headed back inside the castle. As he crossed the courtyard, he watched for the White Wolf. He did not see it. However, it may not show itself to him as it seemed only to be seen by humans.

The demon wondered what would happen if King Hillel approached the White Wolf and tried to talk to it. Would it warn King Hillel about the demon's intentions? Would it tell King Hillel about the consequences of his actions? The demon could tell the

White Wolf the foolishness of this action. It was King Hillel who had called the demon for help in getting to his goals.

But the demon did not want King Hillel talking to the White Wolf. It was not the worry about the White Wolf telling King Hillel the consequences of the actions he has put in motion. The White Wolf could tell King Hillel about many other topics that the demon would rather King Hillel stayed ignorant on. Those were the danger. However, it was unlikely King Hillel would search out the White Wolf. And the White Wolf did not seem to talk to anyone. That lessened the danger.

The demon stepped into the castle and felt better for being inside. He was not sure what about being in the courtyard haunted him, but something did. Perhaps it was the White Wolf, but it was unlikely as the sensation was there before the demon knew the White Wolf was around. The demon shook off such thoughts and feelings. There was work to get done if the plan was to go ahead. Much of the matter was already started, and he had to make sure the rest went smoothly.

The lord from Grackle gave his presentation to the court as scheduled. King Hillel had sat on the throne, trying not to look as bored as he felt. This lord from Grackle seemed to think a treaty between the kingdoms was a real possibility. He talked about the long history of the kingdoms being neighbours and how neighbours help each other out. In all of his presentation, it became apparent that no one had educated this man about the history between the two kingdoms. He did not realize Proster was based on a Prince from Grackle. He did not realize Proster had refused to become part of Grackle.

He was not expected to know that King Zebulon had declared trade with Grackle illegal.

Hillel worked hard not to fall asleep during the presentation. It was long enough and not applicable to anything to do with his life for him give it his full attention. However, he did feel it would be rude to fall asleep. Others in court looked to be having trouble keeping awake. A few looked interested. Hillel noticed that Weldon was staring off into space with no attention being paid to the lord from Grackle.

It was strange to Hillel that Weldon would not be paying strict attention to the presentation. He also paid attention to this type of issue. It was his responsibility to keep Hillel from giving such people as the lord from Grackle credence. He was either lost to his duty or did not think Hillel was taking the lord of Grackle seriously. Taking the lord from Grackle seriously was hard as he did not know anything about the history between the kingdoms.

Hillel thought about the past week and Weldon's behaviour. Something must have been wrong because he had not been bothering Hillel about ruling the kingdom. The courts were still being run, though Hillel did not know whether it was as efficient as usual. At least once in the last two days, the castle steward was wandering around looking for Weldon because he had not been in his office all morning. Hillel did not know what was going on with Weldon, but it had meant that Weldon was not around to bug Hillel about Hillel's duties. It had been a nice break, however, Hillel was wondering if he should investigate the matter to see if it would cause him difficulty later on. But Hillel had little interest in Weldon's life and probably would not recognize what was different now from before.

The lord from Grackle finished his presentation and then waited for Hillel's response. Hillel stared at the man as if seeing him for the first time.

"Is that it?" Hillel asked.

"Yes, King Hillel," the lord from Grackle answered.

"And now?" Hillel asked.

"I need your response to the offer of a treaty," the lord from Grackle answered with the tone that it should have been obvious.

"You are aware that there has never been a treaty between our two kingdoms?" Hillel asked.

"I am," the lord from Grackle answered, "But that is hardly a reason not to have a treaty now."

"Are you aware of any of the reasons as to why there has never been a treaty?" Hillel asked.

"Relations between kingdoms have not been the best in the past," the lord from Grackle answered.

"Nothing you have presented suggested any reason for us to put those reasons behind us," Hillel said.

"At some point, we have to put all those reasons behind us," the lord from Grackle said, "Why not do so now?"

"We will consider your plea and provide answers in time," Hillel said.

"Thank you," the lord from Grackle said with a bow. His face gave away his impatience. He did nothing more than backing away from the throne with his acceptance of his dismissal.

The next issue was brought forward. Hillel paid no more attention to other people rather than the speaker. It was not a matter he cared anything about. Weldon was more aware of this presentation, but not as much as he usually did. Something was different with Weldon. The presenter finished. There was a pause as if everyone was waiting to see what Hillel was going to say. He nodded because he had no memory of what was said, and this no idea what he was supposed to say. The presenter bowed and then backed off, proving his response correct.

Hillel waited for the next person presented, but no one spoke. He realized there was no more business for the day. Rather than just dismiss the court, Hillel waited a moment.

"I have an announcement to make," Hillel said.

There was a murmur among the people of the court, which Hillel waited another moment before continuing.

"We are most happy to announce that Arabella is with a child," Hillel said. This time the response was applause. He smiled.

"Court dismissed," Hillel said. Then he got to his feet. He left the throne room and headed for his father's office.

Weldon stared at the pile of paperwork sitting on his desk. Their presence was not penetrating his mind as was nothing else in his surroundings. The image that held his full attention was a lady in a pink dress with white lace trim and kissable looking lips. She had been wearing other things when she dropped off other letters, but it was the first dress his mind would not let go of. Each visit warmed him while her absence let the cold from the castle seep in.

It was the cold that brought Weldon out and aware of his surroundings, but it was not the temperature of his heart, it was his fingers. Weldon looked around.

Neither of his clerks were there, so no one had started a fire, and nothing was heating the room. Weldon sighed as he got to his feet. He went to the fireplace. As he leaned down to light the fire, the chair beside the hearth squeaked.

Weldon looked at it, but the chair had not moved. The coldness went up Weldon's back and down his arms. He continued to stare at the chair. It did not move for time he was frozen in place. Weldon found himself holding his breath as he listened, but he could not hear anyone else being in the room. A small part of his mind wondered if he imagined the sound but it had been a long time since he had heard things that were not there.

The cold in his fingers reminded him of why he was there. Weldon lit the match and touched it to the wood. Just before the flame touched his fingers, the wood lit. He moved back to watch as the fire spread to the rest of the kindling. Holding his hands up, Weldon let his fingers warm. When they were no longer complaining, Weldon moved back to his desk.

He looked toward the chair again, but there was no sign of movement from it. Weldon moved his attention to the pile of paperwork. He barely got to the second page before his mind wandered off to the lady dressed in pink. A small voice in his mind sent alerts to him, but the rest of his thoughts muffled it.

Hillel's big announcement made everyone happy because the whole kingdom was excited for the heir to be born. But the voice was screaming that something about the announcement was suspicious. Hillel would not have announced anything until Arabella was further along if he was not going to use it for some questionable purpose, which meant Arabella was in danger. She had warned Weldon something would happen. But Weldon was sure Hillel would not endanger the child he had been waiting to have for so long.

The paperwork needed to be done because Hillel would never do any of the work for the kingdom, but Weldon could not think about those matters at the moment. His mind kept going back to the lady in the pink dress, whose father tried to keep her away from the castle. Weldon understood why. The castle itself was not dangerous, and no one had been hurt while there in a long time, but there were dangerous people in the castle. Weldon supposed that if he showed in any interest in the lady in pink in front of others, she would be in more danger and not necessarily by Hillel.

Weldon had never shown interest in any of the women at court as they tended to be shallow and more worried about status than another person. He had wanted a woman who was interested in him and not his position. It also did not help that court fashions had been questionable to him for several years. The one affair he had in his life was with a maid during his teenage years. She had ended it when she met the man she would marry, and he had let her go without objections as he saw no reason to stop her from her happiness. It had surprised her that he was so willing to let her end things, but she accepted with a broad smile.

Now Weldon had met someone who might be worth keeping. But it meant he had to keep her safe from anyone who might want to hurt her. Her father was right to keep her away from the castle, and Weldon had to figure out how to do that while still listening to his own heart. He lived in a house in the city, and it was far enough away to keep her from spending time in the castle, but he spent so much time at the castle himself that he might as well sleep here. The servants he had inherited with the house barely kept it clean and kept up as they found he did not notice much. They thought he had not noticed that they had closed up the half the house he never used, but he had and never said anything because he saw no reason to complain as the space was not used. But if he married, Weldon would expect the servants to have more of the house open.

Married was not something Weldon expected his mind to bring up anytime in the near future, but there is was. He was thinking about how to keep a wife safe and how it would affect the house along with the servants. Despite never meeting her family, Weldon was ready to ask her father for her hand in marriage. When she visited him, Weldon felt she would not have minded if he courted her. The problem was that he did not have much time to court anyone as his job for Hillel took up so much of his time.

Weldon heard the door to his office open. He looked up to see his clerks arriving. They sat down at their desks and started working. After a moment, one of them got up and came over to Weldon to get more work. Weldon picked up half the pile and offered it to the clerk. The clerk took it and went back to his desk with the pile. The other clerk continued to work on what he already had on his desk. Weldon should have been doing his share, but he found himself staring into the fire and thinking about the one thing in his life that warmed his heart.

Hillel was out in the courtyard sparring with one of

the guards as was his usual practice for the afternoon. More people were sitting around and watching this afternoon than usual. He had been ambushed by people since he had made the announcement. Everyone in the kingdom wanted to congratulate him on the baby. He had accepted it all with a smile, but he wished they would all go away and leave him alone. But he understood that this was part of the plan and necessary. He had to look like he was pleased and that there was nothing wrong.

Despite keeping his eyes and ears open, Hillel had not figured out what was going on with Weldon. No one was talking about Weldon and what was happening with him. The main topic of conversation around the castle was the baby. Even those who were not talking about the baby found nothing about Weldon to discuss. Weldon was always busy with the business of the court and never showed interest in much else. Unless he was worried about Lady Rana having left. Hillel was not sure why he would be, but that made more sense than anything else.

Hillel was winning the fight despite his mind being on other matters. This was usual. Sometimes Hillel wondered if the guards were letting him win, but he also knew the last time he caught someone he had punished them. It made him sure they were not letting him win and that he was good. Knowing himself to be good with a sword comforted him and made Hillel confident in the plan going forward.

Out of the corner of his eye, Hillel saw the white wolf. He turned to look and saw the white wolf looking back. No one else appeared to see the white wolf, even the people walking right by it. Despite not seeing the white wolf, no one walked where it was sitting. It was almost like there was something stopping people from walking into the white wolf. Hillel wondered about the white wolf and why it only appeared to him. He wished that book had not disappeared as it could provide answers for him.

The guard smacked Hillel with the sword to remind Hillel about their sparring. He had been too distracted with the white wolf. He glanced once more at the white wolf, but it was gone. Hillel refocused on the sparring. The smack reminded Hillel that the guard was not letting him win, and it was a fair fight. Aside from Hillel being the better fighter, or he was pretty sure that was the case.

HILLEL MOVES FORWARD WITH HIS PLAN AND WELDON DECIDES ON HIS FUTURE

Weldon had faced down angry kings, tavern bawlers, and charging guards, but he was nervous as he sat on a couch in the sitting room waiting to talk to Lady Danielle's father. Lady Danielle and her mother were off shopping for the morning, which was why Weldon and her father had agreed it was a good time to meet. Another reason it was a good time was because Hillel had cancelled court for several days. He did so because he claimed to want to spend more time with Arabella and everyone believed him except Weldon. But Weldon was not going to say anything because he appreciated court being cancelled.

Lord Rafton entered the sitting room. Weldon could see the resemblance to Lady Danielle in his face. Lord Rafton was thinner than most of the older lords Weldon knew, but he did not look sickly. Weldon got to his feet to greet Lord Rafton.

"Good morning, Lord Rafton," Weldon said.

"Good morning, Lord Weldon," Lord Rafton said, "Please sit."

Weldon sat back down. Lord Rafton sat down in the chair across from Weldon. He shifted as if it was hard for him to get comfortable. Weldon did not speak as Lord Rafton as he got comfortable.

"You will have to pardon me," Lord Rafton said, "My health has not been the best, but I hope I am doing better. I hope this matter has nothing to do with my absence from court."

"There are so many who attend I doubt anyone noticed who is there and who is not," Weldon replied, "I am almost more suspicious of those who show up every day than those who miss days."

"There have been many days where I think I should take my family and move to the country estate," Lord Rafton said, "But the doctor was here and refused to move with me."

"Danielle said you did not want her anywhere near the castle," Weldon said.

"I feel it is not a safe place for her to be," Lord Rafton said, "May I ask where you met my daughter?"

"Lady Rana told Lady Danielle to give me any letters for her," Weldon answered, "And Lady Danielle has brought me some letters to send on to Lady Rana."

"Have you heard from Lady Rana?" Lord Rafton asked, "I was sorry to hear she was going to leave, but I fully understand her wanting to go."

"I have received a letter from her," Weldon said, "She said she was having trouble with something trying to kill her, but she was surviving all the attempts. She warned me to keep an eye out for any attempts on my life. She also said there was progress on restoring the estate."

"It is good to hear about the estate, but not attempts on her life," Lord Rafton said, "It would be horrible to lose her. Is your life in danger?"

"I have not had attempts on my life in many years," Weldon answered.

"From what I hear, you have been running the kingdom while King Hillel pays attention to only matters he wants to," Lord Rafton said, "Perhaps he figures that if something happens to you, he would have to do more for running his kingdom."

"There is probably too much truth there," Weldon said, "I did not intend to ever be the one running the kingdom. The only thing I agreed to was to advise Hillel in running King Driscoll's kingdom."

"The problem being that King Hillel wants people to do things for him rather than people to tell him how," Lord Rafton said.

"Unfortunately, King Driscoll did his son a disservice as Hillel has not had to work for anything in his life," Weldon said, "There were servants at the country estate to do everything for him, and he did not even have to make any decisions about running the estate. When he was brought to the castle, King Driscoll tried to teach Hillel about how to run the kingdom, but I do not think the lessons went as well as King Driscoll hoped."

"Well, King Driscoll would be happy to hear about his grandchild," Lord Rafton said.

"He would," Weldon said, "He was waiting to hear that news for many years. I think he was partly hoping he would receive the news before he brought Hillel to the castle. It never happened, and he was worried about it, but there is nothing he could do about that matter."

"It is good that the kingdom is going to have an heir," Lord Rafton said, "But I question any child raised by Hillel."

"The child will also be raised by Arabella as well," Weldon said, "She is a sweet lady, and I would trust her with any child."

"At least this child will have one good parent then," Lord Rafton said, "A child needs that."

Before Weldon could say anything, Lord Rafton started coughing. He coughed a couple of times and then seemed to recover, but then it got worse. Lord Rafton took out a handkerchief and coughed into it. At first, Weldon waited for it to be over. When it got worse, Weldon got up. He went out into the hallway and found the steward coming towards the sitting room. The steward had a glass of water and a bottle in his hands.

The steward went into the sitting room, and Weldon followed him in. Weldon sat back down and the steward handed Lord Rafton the glass of water. Lord Rafton barely got a sip of water between coughs, but one helped to get another. He managed to get a gulp of the water. Then Lord Rafton handed the glass of water back to the steward and took the bottle. He took a large swig from the bottle before giving it back to the steward.

The steward took the glass and the bottle and left the sitting room. Lord Rafton held the handkerchief to his mouth for another moment, but the coughing fit seemed to be over. Weldon waited with concern.

"I am doing better," Lord Rafton said, "But I have not fully recovered. The doctor thinks I will do better once the winter is over."

"It is only autumn now," Weldon said.

"He has ordered me to keep warm," Lord Rafton said, "And I have been trying."

"It does not sound like you are succeeding," Weldon said.

"I do better at times than others," Lord Rafton said, "I thought the cough was going away until this last week. But my health is hardly the worry of anyone else."

"Of course it is," Weldon said, "You are one of those who appreciate that Hillel is not the best king and the kingdom could be in trouble. The thoughts and knowing that are just as important showing up at court."

"But my health is not why you are here," Lord Rafton said, "You said you had a matter you wanted to discuss. I hope it is not something Hillel wants from me."

"It has nothing to do with Hillel," Weldon said.

"So, what is this matter?" Lord Rafton asked.

"I wish to ask for your daughter's hand in marriage," Weldon answered.

Lord Rafton nodded as he sat back to study Weldon. He appeared surprised by the request but not horrified by it. As the surprise wore off, his face took on a thoughtful look. Weldon could feel the urge to explain himself and defend his position, but he kept those thoughts to himself as he knew it would only sound like mindless and nervous chatter.

"There have been others who made that request of me," Lord Rafton said, "I have turned them all down as each time I have had serious concerns about their effect on my daughter's life."

"I understand that," Weldon said, "Your daughter's well-being is important for you."

"My biggest worry about you is that you spend most of your time at the castle," Lord Rafton said, "And I do not want Danielle there."

"I do not want Lady Danielle at the castle either," Weldon said, "I have spent time thinking the matter over, and I realize I practically live at the castle because that is where my life had been. But it is not where I want to spend my life. With a reason to be away from the castle, I will do that."

Lord Rafton nodded. He did not speak as he thought the matter over a little longer. Weldon waited as he knew it was better to give Lord Rafton space.

"My wife and daughter are aware that I have been sick," Lord Rafton said, "But they think I will recover. It may happen, or more likely, it will not. I have been thinking about who will take care of Danielle when I am gone. My wife knows how to take care of herself, and I am not worried about her. But Danielle would be better if she had someone to take care of her."

"If you grant my request, I will do my best," Weldon said.

"I believe you," Lord Rafton said, "My biggest worry is keeping her away from the castle and those dangers. If there have been attempts on Lady Rana's life, you may suffer through those same issues."

"I may have that issue," Weldon said, "But so far, Hillel has needed me to run the kingdom while he ignores those matters. I also plan to keep my job and my life separate. I have not had much of a life before this, and I think I can keep those two apart."

"Are you sure?" Lord Rafton asked.

"I do not want to put Lady Danielle in danger," Weldon answered.

"Did you tell Danielle you were going to ask me for her hand?" Lord Rafton asked.

"I did not," Weldon answered, "I spoke to her once about marriage, and she was agreeable to the matter, but we never discussed it again."

"These last few months I expected her to be sad because her best friend has been gone," Lord Rafton said, "But she has not been. You telling me that she has been visiting you to deliver letters for Lady Rana tells me why. She has been waiting for the right man to come along, and for the first time, I believe she may have found him."

Weldon accepted the statement with a nod but did not say anything. He felt that adding anything more would look poorly on him in front of someone he needed to look good in front of. Lord Rafton let him stew a moment.

"You have my permission to ask her for her hand in marriage," Lord Rafton said.

"Thank you," Weldon said.

"But if she says no, you need respect that," Lord Rafton said.

"Of course," Weldon said, "I would never force my wants on someone else, especially a lady."

"I appreciate hearing it," Lord Rafton said, "But I have heard it before, and the actions of the man did not match it."

"I understand," Weldon said, "I have seen it from others as well, and it bothers me when their actions do not match their words. I try to make both my actions and words go together."

Lord Rafton nodded.

"I can say that now," Weldon said, "But you will see by my actions that I mean it."

Lord Rafton nodded. They were quiet for a moment.

"Would you like to come for supper this evening?" Lord Rafton asked.

"I would accept the invitation," Weldon answered.

"I would like to lengthen this visit, but I need to rest before the meal," Lord Rafton said.

"Then I will go, and I will see you at supper," Weldon said. He got to his feet and bowed to Lord Rafton before leaving.

Hillel was sitting in his father's office and stared into the fire. His mind reflected the flames rather than had thoughts running through it. He had started out thinking about why he had cancelled court, but that had led to questions about the white wolf he had seen every afternoon during sparring for the last few months. Then all thoughts disappeared, and only the fire was there.

The flames were orange and yellow. It was reaching up into the chimney. Hillel could swear the head of the white wolf kept appearing in the flames. The problem was that he was unsure whether he was really seeing the white wolf, or it was just appearing because it was close to the top of his mind. The only place Hillel had seen the white wolf was out in the courtyard, and he had never seen it in the office before. That made it seem the white wolf was just his imagination.

"What are your thoughts?" the being asked.

"Warmth from the flames," Hillel answered, "The

cold from outside has seeped into the castle."

"You are ready for the next piece?" the being asked.

"I am," Hillel answered, "The potion is in the water waiting for her to get up from her nap. It will make her sick, and then the people will determine the next step."

"Good," the being said, "It is too late to back out now."

"I never planned to back out," Hillel said, "I cannot gain my glory if I abandon the plan. It will all go smoothly from here, and I will get that glory."

"Yes, you will get your glory," the being said, "You will be the most well-known king of Proster."

"Of course," Hillel said. Then he knew the being was gone. His attention was back on the flames. The white wolf had disappeared while the being was in the room, and now it was back. This caused Hillel to wonder if the white wolf was there or whether it was in his head.

Hillel settled in to wait. There was no point in going anywhere or do anything. The castle steward would find him when things were happening. Hillel let a slight smile come across his face. His thoughts were filled with his glory found in battle.

Weldon stood in his office and stared at the fire burning in the hearth. His clerks had been working all day to catch up on the matters of the lower court. They had gone to lunch with the rest of the castle servants. Weldon probably should join them, but he was not feeling hungry at the moment. There was a bundle of excitement at the bottom of his stomach taking up space where his hungry usually was. The fire was barely enough to warm the room.

There was a knock on the door frame. Weldon looked over and saw the castle steward standing there with a worried expression on his face. The excitement fell out of Weldon's stomach, and worry filled the space.

"Yes?" Weldon asked.

"It is Arabella," the castle steward answered.

Weldon did not ask any more questions; he just headed for the door. The castle steward led the way. They hurried through the castle hallways and up the stairs. Outside the bedroom Arabella and Hillel shared were two guards and the housekeeper. They moved aside for Weldon and the castle steward. Inside the bedroom, Arabella was lying on the bed. Her eyes were closed. On the floor beside the bed was a glass on its side and a puddle of water around it.

"Arabella?" Weldon asked as he knelt beside the bed but avoided the water. Her eyes fluttered but did not open.

"Should I get the castle doctor?" the castle steward asked.

"Yes," Weldon answered, "And also send for the potion master from the city."

"I will," the castle steward said. He left the bedroom.

"Arabella?" Weldon asked. He gently touched her shoulder. She turned slightly toward him but did not open her eyes. Weldon moved to the water. He sniffed at it, and there was a definite tainted to it.

"Lord Weldon?" a guard had stepped into the room.

"Yes?" Weldon asked.

"What should we do?" the guard asked.

"Stand guard," Weldon answered, "There is little else we can do at the moment."

"Who would do this?" the guard asked.

"Why do you think someone did this?" Weldon asked.

"She was fine earlier," the guard answered, "Then she went for a nap, and a servant brought the water."

"Which servant brought the water?" Weldon asked.

"I did not recognize him," the guard answered.

"Then why did you let him in?" Weldon asked.

"Arabella told us to expect someone to bring her a drink before she went for her nap," the guard answered, "We thought that was the person she expected."

Weldon looked at the guard, who appeared slightly confused and guilty. He understood the foolishness of his actions, but he did not know why he did them. It was like he had been under the control of someone or something else. Warnings flashed through Weldon's head.

"Should I get King Hillel?" the guard asked.

"Not at this moment," Weldon answered, "Let the doctor examine her first."

"Yes, sir," the guard said and then stepped back outside. Weldon looked out and was relieved to see the guard took up his position outside the room. He had been worried that the guard would get Hillel despite what they just talked about. Weldon turned back to Arabella. She was still unconscious.

"Please do not die," Weldon said.

He heard someone arriving and turned to see the castle steward leading the doctor inside. Weldon moved back to let the doctor close to Arabella. He examined her.

"Will she be okay?" the castle steward asked.

"I believe she will be," the doctor answered, "But I

fear her child did not."

The mood in the room went dark. Weldon could feel the sadness come over him. The coldness filled his heart again, and based on the faces of everyone else in the room, they felt it as well.

"Is this what she drank?" the doctor asked, pointing to the puddle.

"Yes," the castle steward answered.

"We will have to wait for the potion master to find out what it is," the doctor said.

"Why will she not wake up?" Weldon asked.

"Knowing what the poison is will help answer that," the doctor answered, "Because it could be the poison or it could just be her body's reaction."

"The potion master has been sent for," the castle steward said, "But it may take a while before she arrives."

"Should we tell King Hillel what happened?" the doctor asked.

"Not yet," Weldon answered. The doctor looked to the castle steward and got the confirmation from him as well.

"Is there a reason we are not telling her husband she is sick?" the doctor asked.

"He is busy with running the kingdom," the castle steward answered. The doctor raised his eyebrows in a question.

There were hurried footsteps from outside the room, and then the potion master stepped inside.

"I came as fast as I could," the potion master said.

"We appreciate that," Weldon said, "Arabella has been poisoned, and we need to know with what and if there is anything we can do about it."

The potion master knelt to the puddle of water and sniffed. She nodded to herself before going through the bag she had brought with her. There was a clinking of jars or bottles, but she brought out a bundle of herbs tied together.

"It is not meant to kill her," the potion master said, "But to make her sick and lose the child."

"Then how do we wake her?" the doctor asked.

"With these," the potion master answered, holding up the herbs. She placed them on a dish and then used flint and steel to start them burning. The potion master waved the dish around so Arabella would breathe in the smoke.

"Getting someone who is not conscious to drink a potion is difficult," the potion master said, "But unless they are dead, they do breathe."

Arabella's eyelids fluttered, and she groaned but did not immediately wake up. It was much slower for her to do that. She opened her eyes and then tried to sit up, but moaned in pain before lying back down.

"What happened?" Arabella asked in a rough voice.

"You were poisoned," the doctor answered.

"The baby?" Arabella asked.

"Gone," the doctor answered. Arabella closed her eyes in pain.

The potion master put the dish of burning herbs on the table and then went back into her bag. She took out two bottles and a small cup. The potion master put a little bit from both bottles into the cup. She swirled the mixture in the cup and offered it to Arabella. Arabella opened her eyes and took the cup. She drank the contents before handing the cup back. The potion master wiped out the cup and put everything back in her bag.

"That should stop the poison from doing any more damage," the potion master said, "But there is little else I can do."

"Thank you for your help," the doctor said.

The potion master left the room.

"I have to get a few things, and I will be right back," the doctor said. He left the room.

"Maybe we should move you out of the castle," Weldon said, "And away from danger."

"How much worse can things get?" Arabella asked as she turned onto her side. Tears leaked from her eyes, and she wiped them away.

"We do not want to lose you," Weldon answered.

"Hillel will never let me leave," Arabella said, "Even if I had a place to go."

"There are places to we can find for you," Weldon said, "And we can do it before Hillel finds out."

"No," Arabella said with a shake of her head, "I might as well stay."

"I just feel like I have failed you, and I do not want to do it again," Weldon said.

"If I feel like I am danger again, I will take you up on your offer of getting away," Arabella said.

"Okay," Weldon said, "Unless you want me to stay, it is probably best if I go."

Arabella nodded. Weldon left the bedroom. He went back down to his office, and sat at his desk. His clerks were not back from lunch, which he appreciated because it meant he was alone. Weldon slumped down in his chair as guilt washed over him. The world was almost crashing down, and he felt like he was not doing his part to hold it up.

She had sat there in his office and asked for his help in keeping her safe. He had agreed to help her. He had aligned himself with her and everything that was not Hillel. He had promised King Driscoll that he would do what was necessary to protect the kingdom and what was good for the kingdom. Instead of protecting Arabella and the heir to the kingdom, Weldon had been distracted by his own life. He even decided that his personal life was just as important as his promises to the man he owed his life to. King Driscoll could have thrown Weldon and Rana out along with their mother and moved along with his life. Instead, king Driscoll had treated Weldon and Rana as if they were his own children. He gave them positions of advisors so that they would have jobs and places in society.

Weldon should have been far more careful of what was going on with Arabella. He should have been paying attention to what Hillel was planning and how it would affect everyone else. Arabella told him she was concerned about Hillel and his plans, so Weldon knew what he should have been doing. He should not have been paying attention to the lower court so much. He should not be happy about the cancellation of the higher court. He should have been concerned about what Hillel was doing when the court should have been happening.

There was the thought that Weldon should cancel his supper invitation, but something inside Weldon refused to send that message. It was a war inside him. He wanted to protect Arabella and the kingdom, but he did not want to do it at the sacrifice of the woman he had fallen in love with. Right now, Weldon did not want to miss supper except if he was really needed here at the castle. He should want to give up his personal life for the kingdom. That was how he was taught. But he could not do that. He wanted to marry Lady Danielle, and he did not want to ruin that with the issues from the king.

Weldon did promise to keep Lady Danielle away from the castle. If he married her, then he would see her at the house, and she would no longer have to come to the castle to visit him. Also, if Arabella needed to get out of the castle, Lady Danielle could help with it and help keep Arabella safe. Hillel might think to look for Arabella at Weldon's house, and if Weldon had a wife at his house, that would be another layer of security. Lady Danielle would be helpful to keep Arabella safe, Weldon was sure. It would also keep Lady Danielle safe.

Would keeping both ladies safe count as keeping his promise to King Driscoll? Weldon thought that maybe it might. King Driscoll never said Weldon should not have a personal life, just that he should do what was best for the kingdom. Protecting Arabella was the best thing for the kingdom. It was a little late to protect the heir. Weldon was going to have to watch where his attention was in the future. He needed to know what Hillel was doing during the times when there should be court. Weldon needed to protect Arabella.

It seemed like Hillel was keeping Weldon busy by leaving everything to do with the lower court to Weldon. Except that Weldon knew it had more to do with Hillel seeing those who came to the lower court as being lower than he was. Hillel did not realize the matters the nobles brought to the higher court meant less than the issues decided in the lower court. The matters the nobles discussed meant little to nothing with the kingdom and more about their personal lives and their wants. The lower court was where the economic issues were sorted out because that was where the merchants and the producers brought their problems. If their issues were not looked at and decided, the whole market of the kingdom could slow or stop.

Weldon sighed and put his head in his hands. He had screwed up, and needed to figure out how to deal with it and not make things worse. He could not talk to Hillel about the matters that concerned him because Hillel did not care about much of it and did not want to reveal his plans to Weldon. There did not seem to be anyone who Hillel did confide in to ask what Hillel's plans were. Arabella had been close to Hillel when they arrived at the castle, but that had changed since King Driscoll had disappeared. She knew some of the plans, which she had told Weldon, but she did not have specifics, and he needed those details. Weldon was not sure how he would get the details, but he was going to have to figure those out.

The door to the office opened, and the clerks came in. Weldon straightened up in his chair.

"Duke Weldon?" one of the clerks asked while the other sat down.

"Yes?" Weldon asked.

"There was some who stopped in to ask when the higher court will meet again," the clerk said.

"That is not my decision," Weldon said, "That is a matter for the king."

"They said he was not answering their inquiries," the clerk said.

"I have no answer for them," Weldon said, "I do not even know how to get the king to answer me. Everything is well with the lower court?"

"Yes, Duke Weldon," the clerk answered.

"That is the important work for you," Weldon said, "Any other matters are not part of your work. Questions on those matters are to be directed to the king."

"Yes, Duke Weldon," the clerk said. He went and sat down at his desk. They looked at each other briefly before getting to work. Weldon thought about explaining the situation but decided they did not need to know. He got to his feet.

Before Weldon could leave the room, Lord Marcus stepped into the doorway.

"Duke Weldon," Lord Marcus said.

"Hello, Lord Marcus," Weldon said.

"I was wondering if you could answer a question for me," Lord Marcus said.

"I can try," Weldon said.

"When will the higher court be meeting again?" Lord Marcus asked.

"I do not know," Weldon answered, "King Hillel has not deemed it necessary to tell me why he cancelled it or when he will hold it again. Perhaps you should seek an audience with King Hillel to gain answers to your question."

"I have tried," Lord Marcus said, "He is unwilling to grant me an audience."

"Then I am not sure what to do to help you," Weldon said, "He is not likely to give me an audience any more than he willing to give to you."

"You are his advisor," Lord Marcus said.

"I am sorry, but I cannot help you in this matter," Weldon said.

"Why is King Hillel not holding court?" Lord Marcus asked.

"I do not know," Weldon answered, "He has not chosen to tell me that either."

"What use are you in this space?" Lord Marcus asked.

"I keep the castle running, so when you show up to complain, there are servants around to listen to your complaints," Weldon answered, "I also deal with traders from other kingdoms, so Proster does not run out of any resources. I know none of those are important to you, but they are to others."

"Very well," Lord Marcus said, "I will seek out the castle steward and see if he can help me."

"Go ahead," Weldon said.

Lord Marcus turned and stalked away. Weldon kept the tired sigh from coming out. He realized the clerks were looking at him. He turned to look at them, and they immediately went back to work.

"He may not get his time in court," Weldon said, "But you need to keep the lower court matters running smoothly."

"Yes, Duke Weldon," the clerks said.

Weldon left his office.

A knock at the door to his father's office caused Hillel to look up from the fire. He looked around as he felt like he had been asleep. The office was empty. He looked back at the fire, and it had burned down. The knock was repeated.

"Yes?" Hillel called.

"Lord Marcus wants to see you," the castle steward replied from the other side of the door. He did not try to open the door.

"Why?" Hillel asked.

"He wishes to know about when the court will be held again," the castle steward answered.

"A few days," Hillel replied.

"Thank you, your majesty," the castle steward said, "You missed lunch, would you like some food brought to you?"

"No," Hillel answered. He waited, but the castle steward said nothing else, and instead, there were only retreating footsteps. He wondered what was going on. The castle steward should have been coming to get him over the matter of Arabella getting sick. She tended to nap but never this long. If Hillel had missed lunch, someone should have already checked on Arabella and noticed that she was sick.

On the other hand, if she was called for lunch, Arabella might not have drunk the water and had just gone for lunch. If that was the case, then she is not sick yet. The guards would expect Hillel out in the courtyard for sparring shortly. If he stayed in the office, it would look suspicious to the people of the castle as he should be going about his day as usual.

Hillel got to his feet and prepared to head out to the courtyard for sparring. He hoped the white wolf would not show up today. It had been distracting him for the last few months, but it never explained why, though he wondered if it had something to do with the being. If it was the case, why would the white wolf stay in the courtyard? Would it not come inside and attack the being? Was there some sort of magic that kept the white wolf out but let the being inside? No one had ever said anything about the castle having magical protection before, so Hillel did not think there was one.

Hillel reached the courtyard, and the guards were

waiting as he expected. He did not see the white wolf, but he never did until he was in the middle of the fight. Hillel decided not to worry about it and got ready to spar. The usual crowd had gathered to watch the fight. Hillel picked one of the practice weapons and a shield that could be strapped to his arm. Then he entered the sparring arena. The guard was already ready and waiting.

This sparring match was the same as every other day. Hillel and the guard battled it out. This time Hillel did not notice the white wolf watching him. The white wolf never appeared. Hillel looked around as usual and expected to see the white wolf, but not today. Instead, he saw Weldon standing on the balcony watching the fight. He was wrapped in a cloak to keep out the winter weather. Weldon was frowning, and Hillel wondered what Weldon was upset about today. It seemed to be Weldon's response to Hillel's existence. Hillel supposed that was how step-siblings were to each other, and it definitely would be amplified with one being a prince while the other was nothing. The only reason Weldon or Rana were anything was out of the kindness of King Driscoll's heart, whether they understood that or not.

It did not matter to Hillel what Weldon thought he was. Hillel never bothered with anything Weldon had to say. They were not related, and Hillel had heard the stories of how mentally unstable Weldon's mother had been, so it was best Hillel knew how to run a kingdom without any of the supposed help from Weldon. But it was best to keep Weldon busy with the business of the lower court rather than trying to kick Weldon out of the castle. Unfortunately, some misguided nobles believed in Weldon, and complain about doing that to Weldon.

Hillel brought his attention back to the fight before the guard could attack. This time he was more prepared. It helped that it was Weldon who was watching and not the white wolf. Because the white wolf would disappear between looks, but Weldon did not move. It did not cause the same strange feeling in Hillel, and he could concentrate better on the fight.

Weldon stood there and stared down at the sparring between Hillel and the guard. The guard was willing to beat Hillel into the ground, but Hillel was good enough to hold his ground. Occasionally Hillel seemed distracted by something, but Weldon could see nothing to distract him.

"He concerns you," the voice from behind Weldon was female. He looked over to see a woman leaning against the railing. He was sure he had never seen her before. Her hair was so light it was white, and her clothes were like none he had ever seen as they were much too tight to be fashionable and a brownish-green colour no one dyed clothing. She looked back at him with bright blue eyes.

"Of course he does," Weldon said, "He is trying to destroy this kingdom."

"No," she said with a shake of her head, "He does not want to destroy the kingdom as without it, he would be nothing. Instead, he wants to make himself part of history."

"He already is as a king of Proster," Weldon said.

"But not in the way he wants," the woman said.

"How would you know?" Weldon asked.

"Because he is taking advice from a demon," the

woman answered, "And the demon is using Hillel's weakness of wanting to be known for something other than just being a king. The demon is the one who wants to destroy the kingdom."

"What kind of demon?" Weldon asked.

"I have not come face to face with it as of yet," she answered, "But Reese says it is a flay demon and they like manipulating humans."

"To gain what?" Weldon asked, "Destroying the kingdom has to gain it something."

"Power," she answered, "There is a source of power here, and it must destroy the kingdom to be able to access it."

"Who are you?" Weldon asked, "And who is Reese? What is a flay demon? What is this source of power?"

"I am a Halden," she answered, "Which is a mixture of elf and dwarf. Reese is a demon of his own type, and he is the only one of his kind. The flay demon tried to hire Reese to assassinate you, but he will not because the Proster line still reigns."

"The Proster line is just about over," Weldon said, "All that needs to happen is for Hillel to die."

"Unfortunately, that is true," she said, "With King Driscoll unable to return, Hillel is the current line, and his death would end the line."

"You know what happened to King Driscoll?" Weldon asked.

"My mother is the portal guardian," she answered, "He is on the opposite side of the portal and unable to return."

"I do not understand most of what you are saying," Weldon said, "How do you know what is happening in this kingdom?"

"Unfortunately, there is a portal in another kingdom, and the guardian of that portal has made a deal with the royal family to let demons through," she said, "And there is a power source here that attracts demons. I do not know what the power source is because I cannot feel it. You would not want to remove it or destroy it because it would change the landscape of the kingdom, and you do not want that.

"My interest in Proster has to do with my family history. Before taking on the guardianship over the portal, my mother was the youngest daughter of King Proster. She fell in love with an elf, and they had me. When dwarf blood and elf blood mix, it creates another being called a Halden. It does not matter how little blood the parents have. The blood should not be mixed, and it only happens when each become bonded with each other."

"I thought that was not possible," Weldon said.

"It is not supposed to be," she said, "Which is probably why it creates a whole new creature."

"You are the white wolf," Weldon said.

"I am," the woman said, "And I have been watching all of you. I tried to warn Hillel about his plans, but he has not been willing to listen due to the influence of the demon."

"He has not been listening to anyone," Weldon said.

"Only because you have not seen him talking to the demon," the woman said.

"I have not seen the demon either," Weldon said.

"It does not want you to see it," the woman said, "Because as long as you never see it, you will have trouble believing it is around, and it exists."

"Based on the changes in Hillel's behaviour since

his father's disappearance, I believe the demon not only exists but is here," Weldon said, "But if it is the demon he is listening to, then we need to deal with the demon."

"It might be best if you can convince Hillel to get rid of the demon," the woman said, "If he understands what is going on, than he will be harder to influence by the demon or any other."

"It might be too late for that," Weldon said, "The demon's plan seems to already be in motion. I am not sure how it is going to end up in glory for Hillel, but something has started."

"All he thinks he needs to start a war is a spark," the woman said.

"He may have that now," Weldon said, "It depends on how he handles what he did."

"What did he do?" the woman asked.

"Kill his unborn child," Weldon answered, "He poisoned his wife, and she lost the child."

"I doubt he is worried about having an heir," the woman said, "He is more worried about his own glory."

"Well, if he is not worried about having an heir, than he will be known as the king who ended the Proster line," Weldon said, "Which would overshadow any glory he earned any other way."

"Which would work well with the demon's plans," the woman said, "That may be how you can convince him to quit listening to the demon."

"I doubt there is any way to convince him to quit listening to the demon," Weldon said, "He probably will not admit that he is taking advice from anyone. Despite King Driscoll telling Hillel to listen to me, Hillel has turned down my advice every time I have offered it. That is why Lady Rana left."

"That is not the only reason she left," the woman said.

"I believe it," Weldon said, "But since she chose not to tell me, I assumed there was a reason for it."

"There are times when I do not understand human behaviour," the woman said, "They are saddened by things that should make them happy, and they destroy things others consider valuable. I would protect any children with my life, but the only way I would have any is if the fates felt they needed me to have one."

"As humans, we do not value life of any sort," Weldon said.

The woman shook her head in confusion.

"If your mother is the daughter of Proster, you should have some human blood as well as the rest," Weldon said.

"I do not," the woman said, "It is not passed on to me; if it has been, I probably would be able to have children and not be able to transform."

"Humans have used magic to transform," Weldon said, "There also items humans can use do that as well."

"I do not need either," the woman said, "Nor, I am limited to how long I can hold that form, and most humans are."

"True," Weldon said, "Humans have more limits than creatures with a stronger connection to magic."

"You are probably closer to magic than the rest of the residents," the woman said, "With an elven father, your blood is more equal parts while Hillel's blood is much more diluted."

"But being raised by humans in a human world, there is a disconnection to that magic," Weldon said, "I do not know anything about using magic. I also know little to nothing about my father, other than he was a wild elf."

"Wild elves here are different from the ones I am used to dealing with," the woman said, "So, I cannot say anything about them."

"I have never been bothered by the fact that I do not know anything about my father," Weldon said, "I have never needed to know anything about him, and I doubt I will ever know."

The woman nodded more to herself than to Weldon. Weldon looked back down at the sparring. Hillel and the guard were still beating at each other. Weldon looked back at the woman, but she had disappeared. It was similar to what happened when he looked away from the white wolf, which he guessed made sense if that was she was. Weldon looked back down at Hillel. Anger filled him at the knowledge of what Hillel did, and he had to take some deep breathes to stop himself from reacting to it all. He turned and went inside before he did something he would regret.

When he was finished sparring, Hillel went into the castle. He headed up to his room to wash up and change. His mind was still sparring and thinking about the moves he should have done to help him win. Only when he saw the two guards standing outside his room did Hillel stop and remember the current situation.

"What is going on?" Hillel asked, "Why are you here?"

"Someone poisoned Lady Arabella," the guard answered.

"What!" Hillel said as he pushed his way into the room. He found the doctor sitting beside the bed and

Arabella lying there. She appeared to have been crying.

"What happened?" Hillel demanded of the doctor as he went to kneel next to his wife.

"She was poisoned," the doctor answered.

"The baby?" Hillel asked, looking at the doctor.

"Gone," the doctor answered, "I am sorry."

Hillel took Arabella's hand.

"Why did you not call me?" Hillel demanded.

The doctor opened his mouth to answer.

"I asked him not to," Arabella answered, "I knew you were busy, and I did not want to disturb you."

The doctor closed his mouth and quickly put a blank expression on his face. Hillel barely noticed as he turned back to Arabella.

"You are my wife," Hillel said, "You should have let them call me. I am never too busy for you."

"I do not want you distracted from ruling the kingdom," Arabella said.

"Your health is more important to me than the kingdom," Hillel said, "Other people can help with the kingdom, but nothing can replace you."

Arabella gave him a small smile but did not say anything more.

"Rest," Hillel said, brushing her hair out of her face.

HILLEL FINDS A REASON TO DECLARE WAR

Weldon was sitting in silence in his office. The hearth was empty and cold as his clerks would not be in for hours. He had not bothered to light any candles or find any other source of light. Weldon was not sure he wanted any light at this moment. He had some light things happen to him, but the kingdom was in trouble, and he was unsure what to do about it. Lady Danielle had agreed to marry him, and he could not be happier about his future with her. He had explained everything to his servants, and they were getting the house ready for other people to live there. There been questions about how much time he spent at home at the moment and whether it would continue. Weldon had assured them he would be home much more.

But things in the castle had gotten worse. Hillel had acted with surprise and anger when he found Arabella and learned the baby was gone. Weldon was unsure what Hillel expected when he poisoned Arabella, but he seemed not to expect to lose the baby. Then Hillel had launched into a whole investigation to find the person who poisoned Arabella.

There was a knock at the door frame as the door was wide open. Weldon could see the castle steward was standing in the hallway with a lit candlestick.

"Come in," Weldon said. The castle steward stepped in and came over to Weldon's desk.

"I was not sure if you were here," the castle steward said, "But the guards at the front assured me you were."

"I had gone home to get some sleep, but I found myself unable to," Weldon said, "So, I came back here. What do you need me for?"

"Hillel believes he found the person who poisoned Arabella," the castle steward said.

"He finished the investigation then?" Weldon asked, "I am surprised he found someone else to take the blame."

"If you think about it, you will wonder why you did not see it," the castle steward said.

"Really?" Weldon asked.

"The poison was found in the rooms of the diplomat from Grackle," the castle steward answered, "And one of the servants who came with him was found to be the person who delivered the cup of water."

"That does make sense," Weldon said, "I had forgotten the diplomat from Grackle was still here."

"He has been waiting for Hillel to call him to court and give him an answer on creating an agreement between the kingdoms," the castle steward said.

"He should have been turned away when he arrived," Weldon said, "Because there was never going to be an agreement between kingdoms, and now Hillel has an excuse to start a war with Grackle."

"Proster does not have a large army," the castle steward said.

"Do you think that matters to Hillel?" Weldon asked.

"No," the castle steward answered, "But it might slow him down."

"I doubt it," Weldon said, "Glory in war is even better when the odds are against one side."

"After a long history of separation, Proster could be taken in by Grackle," the castle steward said.

"At this point, we are short a royal heir," Weldon said, "So, they could make us short a king as well. Have you managed to talk to Arabella and see how she is doing?"

"According to the guards outside her room, she is doing okay," the castle steward answered, "But Hillel has ordered that no one have access to her. The guards are sympatric to people wanting to make sure she is okay, but they are not willing to cross Hillel."

"He is the king," Weldon said, "Despite his attempts to destroy the kingdom he rules and his dismissal of most of the work required of a king, he is still the king. We cannot stop him from declaring war. Not unless you have discovered some way of getting him to take advice."

"No," the castle steward said.

"Anything else?" Weldon asked, "Or can I continue to sit here and contemplate how wrong the world currently is?"

"Hillel is holding court this morning to formally accuse the diplomat from Grackle," the castle steward answered, "I think he plans to execute the diplomat and then let the rest of the entourage go."

"I hope he lets the rest go," Weldon said, "It is best if we do not have to send any messenger from here or even worse, take the bodies back to Grackle. It would be best if he sent the whole group home rather than kill anyone of them, but he wants to show the world how angry he is. I am not sure what we can do about it because he has yet to listen to anyone."

"So, nothing?" the castle steward asked.

"I'm not sure what else there is," Weldon answered with a shrug. The castle steward nodded. He stood for a moment and then nodded again before leaving. Weldon blew hot air onto his hands to try to warm them up, but the coldness had gathered in his bones and would not leave. A fire might have warmed him a small amount, but he did not get up and light one. Weldon felt almost like he was used to the cold. He was not sure whether that was a bad thing or not.

Weldon let his thoughts tumble through his head without stopping any of them to examine them closely. So much going on in his head, and he was not sure the solution to any of it. As much as he knew that he had to come up with something to do about Hillel, Weldon was truly unsure what. He was tired from everything that had happened and the coldness, but he had come to his office because he could not sleep at home. His eye lids felt heavy, but his mind was going a bit too fast.

There was a light ahead of him causing, Weldon to look up. He could not see who was holding to light at first because it was too bright. Then the light moved slightly to the side, and Weldon could see the face of a child. The face was young, and the hair was brown, but Weldon could not tell much else.

"Can you help me?" the child asked.

"What help do you need?" Weldon asked.

"My parents are gone, and I cannot find them," the child answered.

"Where did you see them last?" Weldon asked.

"The courtyard," the child answered.

Weldon took the child's hand and turned to leave the office. They stepped into the courtyard, but something was wrong with it. Instead of the sparring area, there was a platform for hanging people with a pile of bodies below it. Weldon wanted to hide the sight from the child but found instead, the child pulled him towards the platform. They went to the bodies.

"Are your parents among these people?" Weldon asked.

"Those look like them," the child answered, pointing to two bodies near the top of the pile, "But they cannot be."

"Why?" Weldon asked.

"Because their eyes are wrong," the child answered.

Weldon did not recognize the child's parents, but he knew others in the pile. They were nobles who spent their time at court. They were not known to be with the king or against him; they always seemed to be there for the gossip but not to create.

"Next group is ready," a man nearby called. Weldon looked over at the man. It was one of the minor nobles who was always being caught in someone else's bed.

"Bring them out," Hillel's voice came from the balcony. He was sitting on a throne on the balcony where he could watch everything in the courtyard. He was wearing golden robes, and a much heavier crown than any other king of Proster ever had. He also had a

royal spectre.

A group of people were led to the platform. They were chained together, and the guards stopped the group at the bottom of the stairs. Weldon turned away as the first person was unchained and led up the stairs.

"What is wrong?" the child asked.

"I do not want to see what happens next," Weldon answered.

"Have you not been watching the king's demands?" the child asked.

"I have not," Weldon answered.

"How do you not watch?" the child asked.

"This is wrong," Weldon said.

"What does wrong have to do with it?" the child asked, "It is the king's demand for it to happen."

"Just because the king demands it does not mean it is right," Weldon answered, "And right is more important than obedience."

"Right gets you in line for the king's demands," the child said.

"Better to die for being right then live in horror," Weldon said, "A king is still just a man, and a man is flawed, especially when he is giving in to temptation. A king's job is to serve his people, not being served by the people."

"How is a king supposed to serve without being served himself?" the child asked.

A door closed, and Weldon found himself slowly opening his eyes. He was sitting in his office, and his clerks were coming in to work. They had candles to light the room.

"Duke Weldon?" one of the clerks asked.

"Yes?" Weldon asked as he sat up straighter.

"Is everything okay?" the clerk asked.

"No," Weldon answered, "But keep going with the work from the lower court."

"Yes, Duke Weldon," the clerk said. The clerks sat down at their desks and started to work. Weldon felt like his whole body was iced over. He got up and went to the hearth. After lighting the fire, Weldon built it up and crouched down in front of the flames. He stayed there as he waited for the fire to warm him up.

There was a knock at the door, and a clerk got up to answer it. The castle steward was standing there.

"Duke Weldon is needed in the throne room," the castle steward said.

"I will be there in a moment," Weldon said.

The castle steward nodded and then left. Weldon tried to rub the warmth into his limbs. It did not work well, but he did start to feel like he could move again.

Hillel was sitting on his throne and waited impatiently for the rest of the court to arrive. He expected Weldon to be there already, but he had not arrived yet. Hillel and the guards were the only ones in the throne room. The doors were open. Hillel tapped his fingers on the arms of the throne. He was the king; people should be waiting for him. Not him waiting for them.

Weldon entered the throne room. He came to the point and bowed before stepping back to watch. Hillel glared at him, but Weldon did not seem to notice. More of the court came in after Weldon. They bowed to Hillel before stepping back to observe what was happening. Hillel looked over the room and made sure everyone was there.

"I have finished my investigation into the poisoning of my wife, Arabella, which caused the loss of our child," Hillel said.

The room was quiet as they waited for him to explain further. Weldon even seemed to have come to attention. Hillel kept the smirk off his face.

"The servant who delivered her the poison belongs to the lord from Grackle," Hillel said, "And the poison was found in his possession."

Hillel signalled for the guards, who left and brought the lord from Grackle and his servant in chains. The lord looked confused as to why he was here and what was going on. The nobles of the court glared at him. As Hillel hoped, the lord from Grackle was instantly hated by the people.

"You are being accused of poisoning Lady Arabella," Hillel said, "How do you plead?"

"I know nothing of the matter," the lord from Grackle answered, "I am here at the King of Grackle's request to present you with an agreement between our kingdoms."

"Proster has never had an agreement with Grackle," Hillel said, "Except to disagree. What is the real reason the king of Grackle sent you?"

"To bring the agreement," the lord from Grackle answered.

"Has Grackle lost all of its history books?" Hillel asked, "Has Grackle quit teaching history to its children?"

"Grackle still has history books and teach children history," the lord from Grackle answered.

"Then, how do you not understand why there is no agreement between the kingdoms?" Hillel asked.

"But it is all history," the lord from Grackle said, "We can make new agreements and new history between us."

"Or you could be here to sabotage Proster," Hillel said.

"I am not," the lord from Grackle said, "That is not why I am here."

"Then why was it your servant who delivered the poisoned water to Lady Arabella?" Hillel asked.

"If he did, it was not on my orders," the lord from Grackle answered.

"Why was the poison found in your possession?" Hillel asked.

"I do not know why," the lord from Grackle answered, "I was not aware of any poison."

"So, you deny poisoning Lady Arabella?" Hillel asked in a raised voice. He let all the anger from the loss of his child into his voice.

"I had nothing to do with the poisoning," the lord from Grackle answered, "And none of the members of my party were under orders from me to do anything against the kingdom of Proster."

"Then why did you stay after we told there would be no agreements between the kingdoms?" Hillel asked.

"You said I could present the agreement," the lord from Grackle said.

"And you did," Hillel said, "And then you stayed beyond that. We told you when you arrived that there would be no agreements."

The lord from Grackle was quiet. He did not seem to know what to say next.

"We are finding you guilty of attempted murder of Lady Arabella and the murder of her child," Hillel said,

"According to the laws of Proster, the charge of murder carries the sentence of hanging until dead."

"But…" the lord from Grackle started, but the guard beside him silenced him.

"The sentence has been pronounced," Hillel said, "Execute them and sent the rest back to Grackle with the message that if they go against Proster, we will have to retaliate."

"Yes, Your Majesty," the guards said with a bow and then removed the lord of Grackle and his servant from the throne room.

Hillel looked over the people in the throne room. They all seemed satisfied with what just happened. Weldon gave no sign of what he was thinking. No one spoke up or tried to get any attention. Hillel waited a moment longer.

"Court dismissed," Hillel announced.

The people bowed as Hillel got up and left the throne room. He went to his father's office and closed the door behind him. The fire was burning in the fireplace giving heat and light for the room. Hillel sat down at the desk. Today there were no new papers set on the desk.

"That went perfectly," the being said.

"It did," Hillel said, "The people are on my side, and the one taking the blame will be gone shortly."

"The king of Grackle may not respond as you think," the being said.

"Of course he will," Hillel said, "I am going to kill his diplomat, and that is not something he can ignore."

"Good," the being said.

"My glory is coming," Hillel said.

"It is," the being said, "Be careful of your subjects.

Some know what you are doing and wish to prevent you from reaching your glory."

"Weldon will not stop me," Hillel said, "Neither with anyone else. I will make sure they do not interfere with my plans, and if they try, I will turn the people against them."

"As long as you keep an eye on their activities and have a plan to stop them," the being said.

"Of course," Hillel said, "I am ready."

"Good," the being said.

Hillel could feel the being leave. He settled into the chair and looked at the fire. He half expected to see the white wolf, but the white wolf had not shown up in a long time. It was like something was stopping him from seeing the white wolf. He wondered about it and what the white wolf was, but the book was missing and nothing else to help him figure it out. If the white wolf was gone, then it was nothing to worry about and better if Hillel put it out of his mind.

Weldon was standing on the balcony and watching the building of the gallows to execute the lord from Grackle and the servant. It reminded him far too much of his dream caused shivers to go up and down his back. Weldon was already having trouble warming up. It was winter, so his cloak was not keeping out the wind and temperature. The court Hillel had held did nothing to help Weldon warm up despite being in a room with plenty of other people. Weldon had not thought Hillel had figured things out enough to know how to turn the people against someone, but he did it well today.

The gallows was not taking as long as Weldon would have liked. It felt almost like his own neck was the one destined for the sentence. The dream was too close to his mind and the thoughts of the 'king's demands'. How long would it be for Hillel to go from a sentence for a real crime to executing people because they disagreed with him? Weldon already knew that Hillel was the one who committed the crime the lord from Grackle was accused of and sentenced to die for.

It made Weldon wonder what crime Hillel could claim he committed to take him out and not have Weldon around to remind Hillel of the right thing to do. Weldon was sure there was something, especially if Hillel was taking the advice from a demon. The people were currently on Hillel's side because he was only showing them what he wanted them to know. If Weldon tried to tell them otherwise, the people were likely to turn against Weldon. Not that Hillel was a good king, but he had gotten angry over someone the people cared about being hurt.

"Things are worse," Weldon recognized the voice of the white wolf.

"They are," Weldon said, "His plan is starting. The king of Grackle could foiled it, but I doubt it."

"From what I have seen of human kings, they will not leave the insult of killing their diplomats alone," the white wolf said.

"Exactly," Weldon said, "Which means that war is on the horizon. It is a matter of how the king of Grackle responds and when. The group from Grackle has not been sent back and will not be until after the execution, so that they know it did happen."

"What are you going to do about Hillel?" the white wolf asked.

"I am not sure," Weldon answered, "Unfortunately,

he is king, and I am merely an advisor who is ignored. If I appear to be against him, he can demand my head. All he has to do is claim I committed a crime against him or I committed treason. So, anything I do cannot be visible or connected back to me."

"What about his wife?" the white wolf asked.

"She survived the poisoning," Weldon answered, "But now he is keeping her locked up and calling it for her safety, which means I cannot contact her and help her."

"You think she will try anything against him?" the white wolf asked.

"I do not know," Weldon answered, "She asked for my help before she was poisoned, so she may want help before doing anything against him. The castle steward is worried about what Hillel will do and how it affects the kingdom, but he was looking to me to figure out what to do, and I told him I did not know. But if Hillel catches on to the castle steward, he would replace him, and the castle steward is the most likely to be able to help Arabella, so it would be best to avoid that."

"So, you need to figure out how to undermine him anonymously," the white wolf said.

"How do you deal with a demon?" Weldon asked, "Because if we could deal with him, maybe it would be easier to convince Hillel of his foolishness if there was not something telling him different."

"There is a variety of ways to get rid of a demon, but much of it requires magic," the white wolf answered.

"Very little in the kingdom is magic because, for a long time, magic did not work well," Weldon said.

"I suggest you look around and see what you can come up with," the white wolf said, "Because there must be something as King Proster has battled demons, and that means his men battled demons, which means there must be weapons around that would be useful."

"King Proster had a sword he used to fight with," Weldon said, "It was said to have magical properties."

"His sword was borrowed by his daughter when she went after a demon who was stealing children," the white wolf said, "It is not within this kingdom, so you are better off looking to see if any of his men's weapons would work."

"I will have to ask around," Weldon said, "I am not sure who is descended from who anymore. Others who gained titles than King Proster's men, and then there are those who married into those families, as well as families who lost it all and their belongings were sold or given away. But I suppose the castle steward might be able to help me find the resources I need."

"I would suggest talking to him someplace other than your office," the white wolf said, "I believe the demon would spend time there to find out what you are doing against Hillel."

"I suspect as much," Weldon said.

"The only place the demon is not likely to spend time in the courtyard," the white wolf said, "At some point, the courtyard was blessed by a cleric or priest, and it now makes the demon uncomfortable."

"Will the execution change that?" Weldon asked.

"Unlikely," the white wolf answered, "Though multiple would."

"So, we need to figure things out fast," Weldon said.

"It may help," the white wolf said.

"Duke Weldon?" the castle steward asked from the doorway. Weldon turned to look. The white wolf was gone.

"Yes?" Weldon asked. The castle steward slipped outside, but did not immediately say anything.

"That was expected," Weldon said.

"Yes," the castle steward said, "Hillel is letting food into Arabella but nothing else."

"Is he checking the trays?" Weldon asked.

"Depends on the time of day it is delivered," the castle steward answered, "If he is in the area at the time of delivery, he does, but if he is busy, he does not."

"Then there is a way to send a message to her," Weldon said, "It just means being careful about when the message is sent."

The castle steward nodded.

"Are the family trees in the library?" Weldon asked.

"For whom?" the castle stewards asked.

"The nobles who are part of King Proster's men," Weldon answered.

"Yes, those are in the library," the castle steward said, "I can find them and have them delivered to your office."

"I would appreciate that," Weldon said.

"Anything else?" the castle steward asked.

"I would suggest discussions on Hillel as king not take place within the castle walls," Weldon answered, "Out here is fine, but not in there."

"Is there a reason?" the castle steward asked.

"Yes," Weldon answered, "There are listening ears in there and from my knowledge not out here. I think it might be better for our health."

The castle steward thought about it for a moment. Weldon looked down at the men working on the gallows. The castle steward's eyes followed before he nodded.

"Understood," the castle steward said. He turned to start inside before turning back. "Lunch is ready."

"Thank you," Weldon said. The castle steward went inside. Weldon watched the men work a moment longer before going inside for lunch.

Hillel stepped out on to the balcony and sat down in the chair placed there for him. He could see most of the courtyard and especially the gallows. The rest of the court was watching from the courtyard below. Hillel had seen Weldon below, but now he could not see Weldon.

There was some noise, and then a few moments later, the group from Grackle appeared below with guards escorting them. They stopped where they could see the gallows but not in the way of anyone else's viewing. Once they were in place, Hillel signalled to the guards. The lord from Grackle and the servant were brought out and taken to the gallows. The guards separated them at the bottom of the stairs and took the lord of Grackle up the stairs.

The executioner settled the rope around the lord of Grackle's neck. The execution happened. The body dropped to the ground, and a couple of guards took it away. The servant was pushed up the stairs, and the executioner put him in position. Something caught Hillel's eye, and he turned his head slightly. There beside the gates to the courtyard was the white wolf. Piercing blue eyes were focused on Hillel, and it felt like something sharp was entering his chest. He blinked. When he opened his eyes, and the white wolf was gone.

Hillel did not realize he was signalling to the guard until they came to attention. Everyone was suddenly looking at Hillel and wondering what was going on. Hillel struggled to understand what was going on, and then he saw the servant standing ready to hang.

"He has learned his lesson," Hillel said, "Sent him home with the rest."

The guard saluted to Hillel and then released the servant from the noose. The servant was more than willing to join the rest of the people from Grackle. They were escorted out of the courtyard, with several guards going along to make sure they reached the border. Once the group was gone, Hillel got up and headed inside.

Hillel went to his father's office and sat down in the chair. He looked at the fire. His head felt foggy, and he shook it several times to try and clear it. Something felt wrong, but he was not sure what it was. Slowly it dissipated, and he was back to feeling normal again.

"What did you do?" the being asked. It sounded annoyed.

"I do not know," Hillel answered, "The execution of the lord from Grackle went fine, but something came over me when the servant was ready. Suddenly I was acting without knowing what I was doing. It seems to have worn off now."

"At least the lord is dead," the being said.

"We are just going to have to wait for Grackle to respond," Hillel said.

"I hope nothing else gets in the way of the plan," the being said.

"Everything has gone well so far," Hillel said, "One minor slip is not going to destroy the work we have done."

"It better," the being said. Then Hillel felt the being was gone.

Weldon could feel the cold of the wind through his cloak. He kept wanting to find a fire and climb inside to get warm because he had trouble getting rid of the cold since his nap in his office yesterday. It was like it had taken up residence. At least when he tried to sleep at home last night, he did not have any dreams. He appreciated that, even if he could not warm up as much as he would have liked.

There was a sliver of warmth from Hillel's action of letting the servant go. In so many ways, Weldon was sure that Hillel's actions were not planned. But that did not matter so much as the servant still being alive and headed home. Weldon had not wanted the diplomat killed, but one dead over two was progress. Weldon had seen the white wolf, though no one else around him seemed to. But the white wolf was not looking at Weldon and instead was staring up at Hillel. Weldon wondered if the white wolf's presence had anything to do with Hillel's change of mind.

But the white wolf was gone now. She never stayed around for long. Weldon had found himself alone in the courtyard, aside from the guards were who regularly posted. They were much more cheerful than those posted inside. They were also dressed for the weather. Weldon knew he should go inside and get some work done, but he also knew that his clerks were already working and getting things done. They would get things done whether, he was there or not.

Weldon found himself wandering toward the gates to the courtyard. No one stopped him or questioned him as he walked out of the courtyard and into the street outside. He was not sure which direction to go, but he went to the left anyway. His house was in this direction, but he was sure it was his destination. He was seeking warmth; that much he knew by instinct, but exactly where he was not sure.

The thoughts going through Weldon's head distracted him from his journey through the streets. He knew when he was about to walk into anything and go around, but his surroundings, in general, did not get noticed. The streets closest to the castle were quieter than those lower in the city. Most of the people who did walk around were servants of the nobles who were out running errands. It was unlikely to meet any of the nobles as they did not walk from place to another if they did not have to.

"Weldon?" a female voice interrupted his thoughts, causing him to look around. Daniella was coming towards him. She was wearing another light pink dress with white lace. Her hair was up in a fancy braid partially covered by a hat the same colour at her dress. To Weldon, she looked like sunshine on this dark day.

"Hello, Lady Daniella," Weldon said with a smile, "I am just out for a walk."

"Usually, I see you at your office," Daniella said, "Do you not have important business to attend to?"

"My clerks are taking care of most of the business for today," Weldon answered, "I will go back there to do some later. I just needed to get out of there for a while. Things are not going so well at the castle right now."

"Then it might be best if I do not deliver the letter," Daniella said.

"Not today," Weldon said.

"Well, then maybe I will go walking with my beloved," Daniella said with a smile. She slipped her arm into his, and they started forward again.

"I would enjoy that," Weldon said as he smiled back to her.

"Your hand is cold," Daniella said.

"I have been having trouble warming up all day," Weldon said.

"Let us go have tea," Daniella said.

"I would like that," Weldon said. They headed for Daniella's home.

Hillel was sitting on his throne, wondering why he bothered to hold court at all. Weldon could have dealt with everything the nobles were bringing Hillel and expected to sort out, but it was demanded Hillel to listen to the matters and give solutions. Hillel did not understand why they needed him on these matters as if they thought about the issues brought to him, they could solve them for themselves. Hillel looked over the group in the throne room. He did not see Weldon in the crowd. That was strange as Weldon was usually at court, most likely to keep an eye on what Hillel as doing.

It caused Hillel to try and remember when the last time he saw Weldon, and he was having trouble. Weldon was not at the last couple times Hillel had held court, which was strange. Weldon kept such a close eye on things while trying to stay in the background since Hillel had executed the lord from Grackle. Hillel wanted to ask where Weldon was, but he could not do so in the middle of holding court, and it would have looked strange for him to ask about Weldon. It would have made a few people question Hillel and his behaviour.

Before this noble could finish their complaint, some of the guards, who had escorted the group back to Grackle entered the throne room. They did not interrupt things but waited for their turn. Hillel would have to deal with this noble before he could interrupt the court to hear what they had to report. The man droned on and on. Hillel had lost the story long before the guards had distracted him, and things were not making much sense before or after. If it was not for the guards coming in, Hillel might have been close to falling asleep.

The noble started to run down. Hillel noticed that but was not sure what he was supposed to do about what was presented. The noble stopped talking, and everyone looked toward Hillel in expectation of some grand and wise solution. Hillel looked back at the noble in the blank stare sort of way.

"Your Majesty?" the noble asked.

"Yes?" Hillel asked.

"Your decision?" the noble asked.

"Your complaint seems more appropriate for the lower court," Hillel answered.

"I hardly think-" the noble started to say. He stopped at the glare from Hillel. He bowed to Hillel and then backed away. There was no muttering from the nobles standing around watching it, despite a slight shift in the air.

The next person did not step up. Instead, the guards were signalled to go forward. They did without hesitation.

"Yes?" Hillel asked.

"We escorted the group to Grackle as ordered," the head guard answered, "And we received a response from the kingdom of Grackle before we started back."

"And what was that?" Hillel asked.

"King Rafe of Grackle is demanding Proster repay Grackle for the loss of their noble," the guard answered, "King Rafe claims his noble should have been sent back to Grackle for punishment if he committed any crime."

"And what does King Rafe plan to do about it if there is no repayment?" Hillel asked.

"According to the message, he will come to Proster to retrieve it," the guard answered, "If not delivered within the next month."

"We see," Hillel said, "Anything else from the message?"

"No, Your Majesty," the guard said with a bow.

"Very well," Hillel said, "We will contemplate this warning. Court dismissed."

Everyone stood there a moment and then started shuffling towards the door of the throne room. The room emptied slowly, and Hillel sat on the throne waiting. When he did, Hillel did not head to his father's office. Instead, Hillel went to find the castle steward. He found the castle steward was standing in the doorway to the dining hall talking to the head chef. Both men looked at Hillel when he stopped.

"Yes, Your Majesty?" the castle steward asked.

"Where is Duke Weldon?" Hillel asked, "He was not in court today."

"Duke Weldon has been off with his new wife," the castle steward answered, "He is scheduled to be back in a few days."

"Very well," Hillel said. He left them alone and now headed to his father's office.

Weldon arrived in his office after his holiday in the late morning, so his clerks were already working. The fire was going, and it warmed the room, but Weldon had been cold since he stepped into the castle, so it did not help much. The clerks nodded to him and then went back to their work. Weldon looked at the papers on his desk. There were a couple of matters he did have to deal with himself, but otherwise, his clerks had taken care of things.

There was a note just under the first couple of papers. It was from the castle steward, and it asked Weldon if he would meet the castle steward out in the courtyard. Weldon folded the note up and stuffed it in his pocket. Weldon made sure nothing on his desk needed immediate attention, and then he wandered out of his office. He walked through the halls of the castle as if he was not in a big hurry.

Outside the doors of the castle, Weldon found the castle steward talking with the captain of the guard. They were quiet as he approached.

"Are we at war with Grackle?" Weldon asked.

"Not yet," the captain of the guard answered, "But we have orders to be at ready."

"The guards came back with a message from the king of Grackle," the castle steward said, "The king demanded repayment for the life of the executed lord as he felt the lord should have been sent back for punishment if he committed a crime and if he did not receive the money within a month he would come get it."

"Okay," Weldon said with a smile, "I was expecting something like this."

"We cannot disobey the king's order," the captain of the guard said.

"I know and understand," Weldon said.

"But we did not have an army," the captain of the guard said, "And the king does not seem likely to recruit one."

"I doubt he will," Weldon said, "I also doubt he will ask anyone for advice on how to go about going to war."

"And where is he planning to learn about it?" the captain of the guard asked.

"I am hoping he is getting some of the information from books," Weldon answered.

"Books are not the same," the captain of the guard said.

"Unless you can convince him to listen to someone, I am not sure what to do about it," Weldon said.

"I think he is getting advice from someone," the castle steward said, "Because if you stand outside the door to his office, you can hear him talking to someone."

"Is he getting an answer?" the captain of the guard asked.

"Yes, he is," the castle steward answered, "A voice responses to him."

"Have you seen this other person?" the captain of the guard asked.

"No," the castle steward answered, "I thought he was alone each time I have heard the two talking."

"I was told something, but I have been hesitant to share it," Weldon said.

"Why?" the captain of the guard asked, "If you have information that has something to do with the king, it should be shared with those who are tasked to protect him."

"I was told that Hillel is taking advice from a demon," Weldon said, "Hillel wants glory won in battle, but the demon wants the destruction of the kingdom."

"That explains why he was willing to sacrifice his unborn child after he and Lady Arabella waited so long for one," the captain of the guard said, "I thought that had been strange. But if he is more worried about his glory than the kingdom, it makes sense."

"A demon?" the castle steward asked, "But those are just stories."

"It would be nice if that was true," the captain of the guard answered, "But they are real."

"Have you ever faced one?" the castle steward asked.

"Fortunately, no," the captain of the guard answered, "I have family history of stories involving demons. King Proster had fought many during his life, and not all of those were before he ruled."

"He was also supposed to have a magic sword he used to fight them," the castle steward said, "Where is that when we need it?"

"His daughter took it," Weldon said.

"What?" the castle steward asked.

"The youngest daughter took the sword and chased after a demon," Weldon answered, "That was part of why I asked for family histories. I was hoping one of Proster's men would have some weapon useful for taking on a demon."

"Have you had time to look yet?" the castle steward asked.

"I have the start of a list of people to talk to," Weldon answered, "But that is as far as I have gotten."

"If you need help talking with people, I can help," the captain of the guard said.

"Thank you," Weldon said, "The only thing I worry about is whether you will have time."

"We will see," the captain of the guard said, "So far, we are waiting to see what Hillel is going to do."

"Any word on when the king of the Grackle might attack?" Weldon asked.

"A month," the castle steward answered.

"Then we wait," Weldon said.

"Hillel did ask where you were the day the guards came back," the castle steward said, "It seemed to be the first time he noticed you were missing."

"I am surprised he noticed at all," Weldon said.

"He may be thinking you are working against him," the castle steward said.

"Very likely," Weldon said, "I am not worried about it right now."

"Why?" the captain of the guard asked, "He may try to accuse you of something to get rid of you."

"He may," Weldon answered, "And I will deal with when it comes. Right now, I have other things I need to get done."

The captain of the guard nodded.

"I suppose we all have those," the castle steward said with a sigh.

"Then we need to keep things out here and not be seen discussing it," Weldon said.

"Is it because of the demon we should not be talking

about it inside the castle?" the castle steward asked.

"Yes," Weldon answered.

The castle steward nodded with a thoughtful expression.

"If you two will excuse me, I have to get to work on matters left by my clerks that have to do with the lower court," Weldon said.

"I doubt there will be any news until word arrives from Grackle," the caste steward said, "And we will all hear about that when it happens. So, it will probably be a while before we need to talk again."

"I have matters to attend to as well," the captain of the guard said. He nodded to Weldon and the castle steward before going off. Weldon turned and headed back into the castle.

"What is the matter?" Hillel asked the being as he looked up from the book on military strategy.

"Three men in the courtyard and discussed matters," the being said, "You must watch carefully about what they are planning."

"There is nothing they can do about any of my plans," Hillel said, "It is too far along. The only way they can stop the war now it to pay the king of Grackle for the death of the nobleman, and I doubt they can come up with enough for that."

"They have stopped discussion their treason inside the castle," the demon said.

"You make that sound like a bad thing," Hillel said.

"It strongly suggests they have learned things they should not know," the demon said.

"I do not know where they could learn any of it," Hillel said, "No one knows my plan; they just have their guesses."

"They guesses may be close," the being said.

"Why are you so worried?" Hillel asked, "They have done nothing against me as of yet, and the way the plan is working is smooth without many ways for them to mess it up."

"Perhaps it would be good to give them all extra duties," the being said, "Things to make them too busy that they do not have time to disturb things."

"Weldon is supposed to be busy with the lower court," Hillel said, "I will have to send more of the nobles who complain to him. Their complaints are not worth the higher court's time anyway. Who else has been seen out there?"

"The castle steward and the captain of the guards," the being answered.

"Well, the castle steward is going to be busy soon anyway," Hillel said, "Because he will be in charge of inventorying everything in the castle. The captain of the guard will similarly be busy with the preparation for the war. They know Proster is going to war, and they know things needed to be made ready for that."

"Very well," the being said, "But be watchful of them."

"I have not forgotten that they want me to fail in my plan and my goal," Hillel said, "I will not let them do anything to harm me."

The being left and Hillel went back to his book.

The demon settled into the chair in Weldon's office. The fire made the demon uncomfortable, but he knew it was best to sit here and watch over Weldon. The demon always learned more sitting here than anywhere else in the castle. Weldon had his head down as he did paperwork his clerks had left on his desk during his absence. The demon wondered why Weldon worked so hard on the paperwork generated by the lower court. Hillel did not even bother with the lower court, and yet Weldon seemed to think they were just as important as everyone else in the kingdom.

The demon was itchy about things. Hillel had been right about the demon being unhappy about how things were going. The demon had learned about the death of the demon he had sent after Lady Rana and Lady Rana was still alive. Not only that, she was now looking for ways to deal with demons and as well as being in contact with the magician. The magician was a danger to everything the demon had been building in Proster. If he should return, there would be more trouble. Fortunately, no letters about the matter had arrived from Lady Rana to warn Weldon about demons.

It also meant Lady Rana was not likely to come back and if she did not return, the magician was not likely to either. That was good for the demon. Weldon did not know what he was dealing with and was not likely to find out without someone telling him. It made things better for the demon. No one around seemed to believe in demons and would be shocked that they exist. That made it much easier for the demon to sneak around and influence those he needed to influence to gain what he wanted. Destruction of the kingdom was a lot closer than anyone imagined, and the king, who should be protecting the kingdom, was helping to do that.

Weldon put down his pen and stretched. He rubbed his hands as if he was cold. Weldon always appeared to be cold when he was sitting in his office. There were plenty of times when Weldon was alone in the office, and he did not light the fire despite appearing cold. Based on its knowledge, the demon thought that strange for a human, but some humans were stranger than others. The demon watched to see what Weldon would do next, but after rubbing his hands together for a minute, Weldon picked up his pen and went back to work. It seemed unlikely anything would be learned from sitting in Weldon's office, but the demon did not move.

Weldon sat down at the desk in his newly cleaned office of his house. On the desk in front of him were the books of family histories he had borrowed from the castle library and the piece of paper he had started the list of current relatives. As much as he could have thought up plenty of other things to do, but this was important as well. Daniella might have complained about him working outside of his usual hours at the castle, but she was visiting her parents for the evening.

Flipping open the book to the spot he left off, Weldon sighed. The list of descendants was long, and he was far from finished. There were several volumes, and he was still on the first one. He was hoping it would not take the whole month before he could start asking people about the weapons Proster's men left their family. And all of this was just a hope of finding something.

There was a knock on the door. Weldon looked up from the book to see the steward in the doorway.

"Yes?" Weldon asked.

"The captain of the guard is here to see you," the steward answered.

"Show him in," Weldon said.

"Yes, sir," the steward said. He left. Weldon marked his place in the book before leaning back and waiting. It was not long before the steward was showing the captain of the guard into the office.

"Duke Weldon," the captain of the guard said with a nod, "Thank you for seeing me."

The steward left them alone.

"It is not a problem," Weldon said, signalling the captain of the guard to sit, "What can I do for you?"

"I was thinking about what you said this afternoon about looking for the weapons from Proster's men," the captain of the guard answered.

"That is what I am working on now," Weldon said, "I have the start of the list, but I am far from finished."

"I understand, but I think you will not find everything that you are looking for," the captain of the guard said.

"Why not?" Weldon asked.

"Not of the Proster's men became nobles," the captain of the guard answered.

"I thought they all were given titles and estates," Weldon said.

"Not all of them," the captain of the guard said, "Some he let stay as guards and fighting men."

"I suppose there is no record of who and their children," Weldon said, feeling like a weight had landed on him.

"There should be a record of who went which way," the captain of the guard said, "But the records are likely to be in the king's office. As for who their children are, I doubt there is a record of that unless each family has it, and I am not sure how to find those."

"That makes this search much harder than it was a moment ago," Weldon said.

"I am sorry about bringing you this news," the captain of the guard said, "But I felt you should know."

"Do you have any idea how to find some of these people?" Weldon asked.

"There are some who are part of the guards now," the captain of the guard answered, "I have a list of those, but it might be best to be careful about talking to them on the matter." The captain of the guard took a piece of paper out of his pocket and offered it to Weldon, who took it. He unfolded it and smoothed it out. There was a list of names.

"Talking to anyone connected to the castle is going to take finesse," Weldon said, "Some would run to Hillel immediately to report being questioned as suspicious, and then Hillel will use that to prevent the plan from going forward."

"Unfortunately," the captain of the guard said, "There are some men who are ready to follow Hillel into battle against Grackle. I do not understand why they believe him, but I understand they can be dangerous if they find out that I am not fully behind Hillel in his plans."

"We are all walking that careful line," Weldon said, "Which is why I was suggesting we do not meet to talk very often. The last thing we need is for someone to overhear us and report it. I keep hoping we can find a weapon to defeat the demon, and then Hillel will listen to reason."

"That is a lot to hope for," the captain of the guard said, "I am not sure whether Hillel would be willing to leave his ambitions behind and concentrate on being the best king he could be."

"King Driscoll tried to teach his son how to run a kingdom," Weldon said, "But it does not seem like Hillel absorbed any of those lessons."

"He has shown no signs in knowing what it means to be a king," the captain of the guard said, "It is worrisome to all of under him."

"And he wants people to follow him into battle," Weldon said.

"I might not mind too much if he leads the charge," the captain of the guard said, "As much as it is treason to want the king dead, it is easier to leave the battlefield when the head of the charge is taken out first."

"I doubt Hillel will think about gaining glory by sitting on a horse and yelling orders," Weldon said, "Glory comes from leading."

"I hope he believes that," the captain of the guard said.

Weldon nodded.

"I should go," the captain of the guard said, "I will try to talk to the men on the list to see whether they have weapons useful for taking on a demon."

"I appreciate all the help," Weldon said.

The captain of the guard nodded and then left the office. Weldon looked at the list. He recognized some of the names but did not know any of them. If he approached them, they would be suspicious, and it would cause him issues with Hillel. He had enough problems there without adding to them. Weldon went back to looking at the book for the names of people he might be able to speak with.

Hillel was sitting in his father's office when there

was a knock at the door. He got to his feet and went to the door. Hillel opened it to find the castle steward standing there.

"Yes?" Hillel asked.

"There is a messenger here to see you, Your Majesty," the castle steward said.

"I will see them in the throne room," Hillel said.

"Yes, Your Majesty," the castle steward said. He went off.

Hillel stepped out of the office and closed the door behind him. He went to the throne room and sat down on the throne to wait. It was not long before Weldon showed up and stood to one side. Hillel would have been more suspicious if he had not shown up. A guard showed up with a man in a uniform from a noble house Hillel did not immediately recognize but looked like one from near the border to Grackle. The messenger stopped and bowed.

"Yes?" Hillel asked.

"I was sent by my master to inform you that an army is gathering across the border in Grackle, Your Majesty," the messenger answered, "They look like they are getting ready to attack."

"I appreciate your master's message," Hillel said, "You may head back. You can tell your master I will send men to protect Proster from any invasion."

"Yes, Your Majesty," the messenger said with a bow. Then he left the throne room. The guard did not immediately follow him.

"Send for the captain of the guard," Hillel said.

The guard bowed and then left the throne room. Hillel waited as did Weldon. They did not speak, and Weldon did his best to pretend to be part of the decoration. Hillel did not care as there was nothing Weldon could do stop things now.

The captain of the guard arrived and bowed to Hillel. He did not even glance at Weldon.

"You requested my presence, Your Majesty?" the captain of the guard asked.

"Yes," Hillel answered, "We need a group of men ready to go into battle against the king of Grackle. They must be ready the morning a day from now."

"Yes, Your Majesty," the captain of the guard said with a bow. He left the throne room. Weldon did not move.

"We suppose court should be called," Hillel told Weldon, "As well as the castle steward."

"Yes, Your Majesty," Weldon said. He bowed and then left the throne room.

Hillel waited. He tried not to let the smugness show on his face. Everything was going to plan exactly as he thought they should. No one could fault him for defending the kingdom against attack, especially when the other kingdom started it. His name would go into history books as a king who did not turn away from a fight.

Nobles started coming into the throne room. They settled into their usual positions around the room. Weldon came back in and moved back to where he had been standing. Then the castle steward entered. He came and bowed to Hillel.

"You have a request of me, Your Majesty?" the castle steward asked.

"Yes," Hillel answered, "I have an announcement to make and from that a need for you to fill."

"Yes, Your Majesty," the castle steward said with a

bow. Hillel had everyone's attention.

"We received a message from the border that Grackle's army is gathering at the border," Hillel said, "As such, Proster is at war. We will take men to defend our kingdom soon, and we expect support from all subjects."

There was nodding from the nobles in court at this pronouncement. The castle steward stood and waited.

"We need you, the castle steward, to prepare supplies to go with us," Hillel said.

"Yes, Your Majesty," the castle steward said, "It will be ready when you are."

"Court dismissed," Hillel said.

Everyone bowed and then shuffled out of the throne room. Hillel watched them all leave before moving from the throne. Weldon had left with everyone else, but he had shown no expression or emotion as to the events that just happened. Hillel might have been concerned about Weldon and what he could do, but Weldon could not stop Hillel's plans. Hillel went back to his father's office to prepare himself for going to war.

Weldon stood on the balcony and looked over the courtyard. The captain of the guard was getting men ready as ordered to do so by Hillel. The captain of the guard did not seem to be going himself, and since Hillel did not specify that the captain of the guard was going, it was understandable.

"So, he did do it," the white wolf said from beside Weldon.

"Yes," Weldon said, "But it was expected as soon as he executed the lord from Grackle for a crime he committed himself."

"And he still believes it will gain him glory," the white wolf said.

"He does," Weldon said, "What else is war supposed to do?"

"Kill men who go," the white wolf answered.

"He is not thinking about that," Weldon said, "He seems to feel that as the king of Proster, he is invincible and as such, he is in no danger. The only thing he thinks will happen is his glory will be shown to the world. Historians will write about his great deeds for centuries to come."

"The demon will not be going with him to war," the white wolf said.

"I figured," Weldon said, "He cannot continue his plan for destruction if he goes with Hillel. I have not stopped trying to find a weapon, but it is slow trying to figure out who is descended from Proster's men. I cannot question them until I identify them."

"There are no stories about other weapons such as Proster's sword?" the white wolf asked.

"Not that I have heard," Weldon said, "But I was never very interested in weapons for much of my life and my sister and I did not spend a lot of time with other nobles' children. We were considered outsiders by many, except Driscoll."

"That does make it harder to hear stories from families," the white wolf said.

"Fortunately, I am more accepted now and can talk to people," Weldon said, "Once Hillel leaves, I can talk to people without hiding as much."

"The demon will still be here and will work against you," the white wolf said.

"The demon will do that," Weldon said, "But I am hoping I can figure out how to deal with it before it figures out how to stop me. When Hillel is gone, the demon cannot convince Hillel to execute me."

"He can convince others to turn on you," the white wolf said.

"That is true," Weldon said, "But if I worry too much about it, I will be distracted from what I need to do."

"But you need to watch out for it," the white wolf said.

"I am aware," Weldon said, "But I cannot let it distract me from attempting to find a way to destroy the demon. It can do more damage if I leave it than if it is dealt with."

"There is that," the white wolf said.

"You know the demon is here," Weldon said, "Why can you not help with this matter?"

"I am not supposed be here at all," the white wolf said, "So if I interfere with matters here, it will cause more trouble than one demon. I am not sure why I keep visiting, but for some reason, I feel a connection to this kingdom and the royal family."

"Because you are related to them," Weldon said, "You are a closer relation to them than I am."

"I grew up in a world where family did not mean much," the white wolf said.

"Maybe you are searching for family," Weldon said, "Just because you are not human does not mean you do not crave the connection of family. The problem is that Hillel is the current member of the family available, and you can see that you will never have a connection with him, so you are trying to solve the problem that is Hillel and his destruction."

"I suppose that sounds about right," the white wolf said, "But it lacks the logic I am used to."

"But does logic have to do with the actions of people, no matter what kind?" Weldon asked, "I have never noticed that true logic has nothing to do with actions, except the logic the person thinks might work."

"I know some beings who do not act unless it is logical to do so," the white wolf said, "But they are cold and calculated and lack any warmth about them. I never assumed myself as logical as they are, but I did not think I was overly connected or looking for it."

"Maybe someday there will be a king of Proster who you can connect with," Weldon said, "That is if the Proster line manages to continue. That is highly questionable at this point."

"When Hillel leaves, I will have to go as well," the white wolf said, "And I will not be back unless there is another of the line of Proster."

"Understandable," Weldon said, "If your connection is to the family, then why would you be here if they are not? I will continue to work on defeating the demon and defending the kingdom from those who would destroy it. That is my job."

"It will probably be easier once Hillel is off at war," the white wolf said.

"Partly," Weldon said, "We will see what the result of the war is. Maybe the war will teach him a lesson, or it might take him out entirely. I am not sure what happens if he dies."

"I do not know what the rules are here in Proster," the white wolf said, "But most kingdoms have a line of people who get the throne and what order."

"I would have to look," Weldon said, "If something happens, people will look to me to have the answers because that is my job."

"Driscoll never told you what to do if Hillel dies?" the white wolf asked.

"He assumed it would not be necessary," Weldon answered.

"His assumptions may be the downfall of the kingdom," the white wolf said.

"They are," Weldon said, "But he meant well, and he thought he had taught his son the right thing to do. He did not expect his son to have different ideas than he did."

"Never assume others have the same ideas you do," the white wolf said.

"I find that it happens when many parents," Weldon said, "They believe their children are blank books until the children show themselves as individuals, and Hillel never showed his personality to King Driscoll. No one knew what Hillel would bring to being king until King Driscoll was gone, and Hillel took over. Even his wife, Arabella found he had a change in personality when he became king."

"Power has been known to do that to people," the white wolf said.

"It does," Weldon said, "I would to not be one of those people, but I could be wrong."

"You were given lessons by Driscoll to help rule," the white wolf said, "And you have seen what he was doing wrong. You should be better in power than he has been."

"I also know that I do not want to be king," Weldon said.

"Usually, a good sign that the power would not go to your head," the white wolf said.

"Or a sign that I know I would be a poor leader," Weldon said, "And I know my limits."

"There is that possibility," the white wolf said.

The captain of the guard was sorting through a group of men. Some of them seemed to be trying to catch his eye as if volunteering for the jobs he was giving out. Weldon could not hear what the captain of the guard was saying, and that left Weldon wondering if they were volunteering to stay and guard the castle or go off to war with Hillel.

"Hillel should not have caused the death of his child," Weldon said, "It causes too many problems for everyone else."

"That is what happens when a king thinks only of himself," the white wolf said.

"Unfortunately," Weldon said.

There was a shuffling from the doorway behind Weldon caused he to glance back. The white wolf had disappeared. However, he could not see anyone at the door. Weldon went to the door and opened it to look around. He did not see anyone, but he did feel a cold that had nothing to do with the temperature outside.

Weldon stepped inside and closed the door behind him. The hallway was empty. He headed toward his office. Weldon did not meet anyone in the hallways, but there were moments when he heard footsteps behind him. Occasionally he would attempt to see behind him as carefully as possible, but Weldon could not see the person back there. They were either good at hiding, or they were invisible.

The thought went through Weldon's mind that it was

demon following him, but Weldon dismissed it. He had felt like the demon had been watching him for months, and it did not feel like this. It was much colder, and there was a tingling on the skin. This was the feeling of being watched and the sound of footsteps. It also lacked that malevolent presence Weldon has sensed before. The coldness he had felt entering the castle seemed to everywhere and not just in one place, also when he was walking through it and not having it generate behind him.

Weldon reached his office and went inside. At first, Weldon thought the footsteps did not follow him, but then he heard the quiet shuffling of someone moving around and trying not to make noise. Weldon sat down at his desk. He was about to get to work when he noticed his clerks exchanging looks and then glancing at him before pretending to work.

"Is there something wrong?" Weldon asked.

"We were wondering if King Hillel will conscript an army, Duke Weldon?" the one clerk said while the other one nodded.

"It does not seem likely," Weldon answered, "He is leaving the morning after tomorrow, and that hardly seems like a good time to start demanding people join an army. I am sure that if you have training with a sword and are interested in volunteering, you would be accepted."

"We just wanted to know if we needed to tell our wives that we would be recruited into the army," the other clerk said.

"So far, there has been no suggestion of conscription," Weldon said, "But it is still possible."

The clerks nodded as they accepted what he said.

Then they went back to their work. Weldon left them to it. He had never thought about conscription, and as far as he could tell, neither had Hillel. That was a good thing as the less innocent men would be going into battle with him. Weldon did not doubt there would be volunteers who joined Hillel and his men.

There was a knock at the door of the office. Weldon looked over and saw the castle steward standing there. He looked a little ragged. Weldon got to his feet and went out into the hallway.

"I have been trying to get everything together for King Hillel," the castle steward said as he led the way, "But there have been several people from the town arrived at the door to the lower court, and the guards keep referring them to me, and I do not know what to do with them because I do not have time to listen to them. I told the guards to get you, but they seem to have a hard time listening."

"What is going on with them?" Weldon asked.

"They did not seem very happy about the situation," the castle steward answered, "I think a few of them are trying to avoid the captain of the guard. I am not entirely sure, but I think one had disappeared from his post."

They entered the main entrance. They found the captain of the guard standing there.

"There you are," the captain of the guard said to the castle steward.

"I was going to find you next," the castle steward said, "But first I had to get Duke Weldon."

"Does that have to do with the line of townspeople gathering?" the captain of the guard asked.

"It does," the castle steward answered.

"Good," the captain of the guard said, "They are getting in the way of some of my men."

"I think some of your men are disappearing or avoiding you," the castle steward said.

"I figured as much," the captain of the guard said.

"My clerks were asking about conscription," Weldon said.

"I have no orders on conscripting anyone into the group going with King Hillel," the captain of the guard said, "I have been mostly collecting volunteers. Once I have all of those together and see how many there are, then I will start picking who to add to the group."

"And if others volunteer?" the castle steward asked.

"Send them to me once you know whether they can handle a sword or other weapons," the captain of the guard answered, "The last thing I need to send with King Hillel is men who cannot fight. Enthusiasm is great, but cheerleaders are useless."

"Okay," the castle steward said with a nod.

"Can something be done about the line of people?" the captain of the guard asked.

"I will go see about it now," Weldon answered, "Where is King Hillel at the moment?"

"He has locked himself in his study," the castle steward answered, "He asked not to be disturbed."

"Okay, then we will not disturb him," Weldon said. He left the castle steward and the captain of the guard to finish their discussion. He went to where the lower court was held. He found a couple of guards standing in the hallway outside.

"Good, you are here," Weldon said as if he expected them to be there, "We will let the people in and hear what they want."

"Yes, Duke Weldon," the one guard said as they both nodded. They both looked like they were relieved to have a job they were needed for. Apparently, the guards had not been informed that the captain of the guard was looking for volunteers.

Weldon opened the doors to the lower court and took his seat behind the desk. The guards closed the doors into the castle and then opened the doors into the courtyard. The line entered and filled up the audience area. Weldon waited until the shuffling was over and most of the people were inside before clearing his throat. The people quieted down. The first person stepped up.

"What matter are you bringing today?" Weldon asked.

"I wish to volunteer to fight alongside our king," the man answered.

"What qualifications do you have?" Weldon asked.

"My father was a member of the guard," the man answered, "He taught me how to fight. I am part of the watch when I am not working in my shop."

"Do you have equipment?" Weldon asked.

"I do," the man answered, "My father passed his down to me when he died, and I have kept it in the same shape so that it is ready to go into battle at any time."

"Report to the captain of the guard," Weldon said.

"Thank you, Duke Weldon," the man said with a bow. He left, and the next person took his place.

"What matter are you bringing today?" Weldon asked.

"I want to know why the king is taking this kingdom to war," the man answered.

There were boos and disses from the audience. Weldon held up his hand, and the people quieted.

"Proster is going to war in response to Grackle," Weldon said, "The king of Grackle has men at the border ready to attack, and King Hillel will be riding out to meet them."

"But what about this kingdom?" the man asked, "There is no heir."

"That is not a matter King Hillel has seen fit to share with us," Weldon said, "But I am sure he has figured it out."

The man opened his mouth, but one of the guards touched his arm and escorted him out. The next person stepped up.

"What matter are you bringing today?" Weldon asked.

"I am a farmer," the man answered, "And I willing to provide supplies to the men going into battle."

"Tell me what supplies you are willing to provide, and I will pass it along to those who are packing those," Weldon said.

The man listed it, and Weldon wrote it down along with the man's name. Then the man bowed and then left. The next person stepped up.

The main points from the people were either supplies or volunteering to go to battle. Weldon took down the list of supplies and names to pass along to the castle steward. He asked for qualifications before sending anyone to the captain of the guard. If they could not list any qualifications, Weldon suggested that they gain some before the possibility of being sent into battle. Most of them accepted those conditions and asked that their names be listed should there were training offered. One or two tried to argue that the king needed their help now, but Weldon refused to send them to the captain of the guard.

It was supper time by the time Weldon finished with the lower court. He supposed more people would be there tomorrow, but he was not going to worry about that. Weldon closed the lower court, dismissed the guards, and then headed back to his office. He could still hear the footsteps behind him but still could not see whoever it was. They did not seem to be a danger to him, and so he ignored them.

Going through the main entrance, Weldon came across the castle steward who was standing there with a list in his hand and looked like it had been a long day.

"What did people want?" the castle steward asked when Weldon stopped next to him.

"To help out the king with his war," Weldon answered, "I sent those with qualifications to fight to the captain of the guards. Here is a list of people who are willing to provide supplies." Weldon offered the list to the castle steward, who accepted it and looked over it.

"This should fill in the gaps I have," the castle steward said, "I appreciate this."

"You can thank the people who offered," Weldon said.

"I will," the castle steward said, "Supper is ready in the dining room."

"I am going to eat at home," Weldon said.

"Of course," the castle steward said.

"I will be back early tomorrow," Weldon said, "If any more people show up, tell them the lower court will be open tomorrow mid-morning."

"I will," the castle steward said, "Good night."
"Good night," Weldon said. He left the castle.

HILLEL GOES TO WAR

Hillel smiled at the sight of the men standing at ready as the sun came over the mountains and into the courtyard. They were all ready to follow him into battle. He was unsure where the captain of the guard found so many, but Hillel was glad for the amount. He let the smile fade as he went back inside. Hillel went through the hallways down to the main entrance. The castle steward, Weldon, and several other servants were waiting to see him off. All of them bowed as he walked by, and he nodded to them.

Outside the doors, his horse was waiting for him. Hillel used the steps to mount. Then he rode out to sit in front of the battalion of men. He did notice some of the men were not in the same uniform as the guards from the castle and realized some of the men were residents of the town, which Hillel was more than willing to accept.

"Men," Hillel raised his voice so everyone could

hear him, "We are now heading to battle the kingdom of Grackle. We are responding to their threats. We are defending our kingdom. We will not let these insults stand. We will defeat this threat. We will return victorious."

The men roared with support of every point. He had their full support. This time he let the smile pull the corners of his mouth. He raised his arm and yelled with the crowd. Then he let his arm lower, and the men settled down.

"Let us go to war," Hillel said. There was another shout, and then everyone prepared themselves to leave. Hillel got his horse moving toward the courtyard gates. The men fell in behind him, and the supplies wagons came behind them.

Outside the gates, the streets were lined with cheering crowds of people. Hillel waved as he rode passed them. The scene was exactly as he had imagined. Everything was perfect. It was going to be even better when he returned victorious, but this would work until then. It was great that his people supported him.

Hillel remembered when he got ready this morning. Arabella had begged him to reconsider this war and riding into battle. She had asked him to stay and told him that this whole war was foolishness and that he did not need to do this. If he wanted glory, it would be better if he was a great and wise king. He had tried to explain to her the other day that he needed to do this, and this was important to him. So, he had explained his main points again and then told her he would be back soon.

Weldon had not looked like he supported Hillel

going off to war. The castle steward also appeared not to be supportive. However, they both helped him prepare to leave. The captain of the guard had shown no sign of being against it and had gotten the men together as ordered. Hillel had not ordered the captain of the guard to come, so the captain of the guard was not among the men marching behind him. Hillel would have told him to stay if he had been part of the group as Hillel would not gain as much glory for being victorious if others were leading the men.

Everything was working out at Hillel had planned. He was going off to his glory. His supporters were cheering him on. His men were marching behind him. It was going to be great. Hillel reached the gates of the city. The guards on either side came to attention as he passed. He nodded to them and then rode out of the city. His glory was waiting.

Weldon was standing on the balcony with the castle steward and the captain of the guard. They had been watching Hillel's army go through the streets for as long as they were in sight.

"That was a lot of men," the castle steward said.

"I was quite surprised at how many volunteers there were," the captain of the guard said, "But the more volunteers meant less of my men needed. I think more of my men will reappear today now that they are not worried about being sent off to war."

"They are the guards; they should not be so cowardly in the face of battle," the castle steward said.

"The castle guards have had a pretty safe life so far," Weldon said, "There have been too many years since they have had to go into battle. They thought they had signed up to protect the king and not be members of the army."

"I suppose that makes sense," the castle steward said, "But it seems strange to me that they would disappear like they did to avoid battle. If Grackle invades and reaches the castle, they will have to join the battle."

"That is true," the captain of the guard said, "But hopefully it does not come to that."

"You think that many men will stop Grackle from invading?" the castle steward asked.

"It is possible," the captain of the guard answered, "We will find out."

They stood there without talking for several minutes. The sun warmed the stones, but it was not enough to counteract the coldness of the wind. Weldon still found it warmer outside than inside the castle.

"Who becomes king if Hillel does not come back?" the castle steward asked.

"I have been asking myself that question," Weldon answered, "But I have not found the answer yet. I think the book is in Hillel's office."

"I would never have tried to go look for it before," the castle steward said, "But it likely safe with Hillel gone."

"I will look into it today," Weldon said.

"We cannot hope the demon followed Hillel off into battle, could we?" the castle steward asked.

"The demon's goals have nothing to do with Hillel's battles," Weldon answered, "The demon's goal is the destruction of the kingdom and to do that, it needs to be here."

"So, we still need to keep trying to figure out how to

defeat it?" the castle steward asked.

"Yes," Weldon answered, "But with a battle going on, people are likely to assume we want to send the weapon on to Hillel to help him defeat Grackle."

"I was going to start to ask about it the other day, but then Hillel wanted men gathered," the captain of the guard said, "I will get to it today."

"I appreciate that," Weldon said, "Part of my plan is to start questioning my list of people. The lower court will not be held today. Anyone who shows up can be sent away and told to come back tomorrow."

"I suppose we should all get on with our work," the castle steward said.

"If someone needed us, they would come and interrupt," Weldon said.

"No one had been shy about doing that," the captain of the guard said.

Before anyone could say anything else, they heard the balcony door open. They looked back and saw a guard standing there. He was one of the ones who had the job of guarding Lady Arabella.

"Lady Arabella has requested Duke Weldon and the castle steward's presence," the guard said.

"We are coming now," Weldon said.

He and the castle steward followed the guard inside. The three of them went up to Arabella's room. The other guard was still standing outside the door. Weldon and the castle steward went inside while the guard took up his position on the other side. Lady Arabella was dressed and sitting on a chair, waiting for them.

"I am assuming Hillel is gone," Arabella said.

"He is," Weldon said, "I did not know if the guards are willing to let you leave or whether they are going to hold to Hillel's orders."

"I have already talked to them," Arabella said, "They are willing to let me leave, but only if one of them comes with me to keep me safe."

"I think your safety is not as much of a concern with Hillel gone," Weldon said.

"You are correct," Arabella said, "But few people believe that matter, and so they are still worried about such things. I am not going to argue with them on the matter because they are letting me out. I am excited to wander the castle again."

"It is cold where there is no fire to warm you," Weldon said, "But it is much bigger than this room."

"Then let us walk for a while," Lady Arabella said as she got to her feet. She led the way out of the room. Weldon was half a step behind her and the castle steward a full step. The two guards walked behind the three of them.

"Hillel said you had disappeared for a few days," Lady Arabella said to Weldon.

"I was gone for a couple of weeks," Weldon said, "I took the time away to spend with my wife after our wedding."

"You are married now?" Lady Arabella asked.

"I am," Weldon answered.

"Wonderful," Lady Arabella said, "She must come to tea someday soon so I can meet her."

"Whenever you are ready, I will deliver the invitation," Weldon said.

"Any other news?" Lady Arabella asked.

"Most of the usual things," Weldon answered.

"Have you heard from Lady Rana?" Lady Arabella asked.

"I did receive one letter from her," Weldon answered, "She was doing well, but there were a couple of matters she was concerned about. She warned me to be careful."

"She did not have any other news?" Lady Arabella asked.

"Not that she wrote in the letter," Weldon answered, "Were you expecting her to share some other news?"

"I am expecting other news from her," Lady Arabella said, "But I suppose I would have to write her myself to hear about it."

"Very likely," Weldon said, "I do not know the matter you are asking about it, so I cannot ask her."

"What does she think of your marriage?" Lady Arabella asked.

"I have not heard from her since before the wedding," Weldon answered, "I keep hoping to receive another letter any day."

"I hope one comes soon," Lady Arabella said, "It would be nice to hear how things are coming along with her."

"It would," Weldon said.

They reached the doors to the balcony. Lady Arabella opened them, and everyone followed her out. The captain of the guard was no longer there. The guards took up positions on either side of the doors.

"We have a problem," Lady Arabella said in a lower voice so the guards could not hear.

"Which one is that?" Weldon asked in a quiet tone.

"I did not realize it before, but Hillel has been taking advice from the wrong type of being," Lady Arabella answered, "And it was that being that suggested poisoning me and gave him the recipe. I know it did not leave with him."

"We have been warned about it," Weldon said, "And we have been searching for a weapon to destroy it."

"Good that we all know," Lady Arabella said, "But I should mention that I am not completely safe just because Hillel is gone. The being is good at manipulating people and convincing them that they will get what they want if they help it get what it wants."

"The guards are not going to let you alone," Weldon said, "If you need anything else, we find a way to provide it."

"I have a question," Lady Arabella said.

"Ask," Weldon said.

"If Hillel dies, what happens to the kingdom?" Lady Arabella asked.

"People keep asking me that," Weldon answered, "But I have not had time to look up the answer. It is in a book in Hillel's office, and until today, I have hesitated to go in there."

"Would King Driscoll tell you?" Lady Arabella asked.

"He did not because he expected Hillel to survive and provide an heir," Weldon answered, "Everything was supposed to be set before Hillel died. If Hillel left an heir, they would be in line to be the next king even if someone else has to rule until the heir comes of age."

"Has Proster ever had a queen?" Lady Arabella asked, "I have never heard of one, and when Hillel was announced as king, I was announced as consort."

"Proster's wife was queen, but no other king has had a queen," Weldon answered, "No woman has been in line for the throne as there had always been a male on the throne or a male heir available. That is not to say there cannot be one, so much as there has not been one."

"Few people are very accepting of changes like having a queen when there had not been one in generations," Lady Arabella said, "Especially if none have been in control of the kingdom. As Hillel's step-brother, would you not be in line for the throne next?"

"I doubt the subjects would be any more welcoming of me taking the throne than you taking it," Weldon answered, "I am not of Proster blood."

"What I know of the Proster line it is over with Hillel," Lady Arabella said, "So, where does that leave the kingdom without a king?"

"You are right about Hillel being the end of the line," Weldon said, "And I need to look up the information before I can answer questions about it."

"Then, we may have to make a time to meet and discuss matters," Lady Arabella said, "Because I am not sure that Hillel will come back."

"He had a lot of men with him," the castle steward said.

"But he has never been to war, and he is not going to take any advice because it would take away from his glory," Lady Arabella said, "I have read enough history to know that people who head into war with that mindset usually do not return home alive."

"We can meet for tea in a couple of days at my house," Weldon said.

"Sounds good," Lady Arabella said, "Thank you for walking with me."

Lady Arabella turned and went inside. The guards followed her.

Weldon gave her a minute before turning to the

doors. The castle steward came with him. Once in the hallway, Weldon could hear the footsteps behind them. They were not as loud today, but Weldon could hear them.

"There is someone following us," the castle steward said.

"They have been following me for several days," Weldon said, "But I cannot see them, only hear them."

"Could it be the demon?" the castle steward asked.

"I doubt it," Weldon answered, "I think the demon moves much more quietly. I am sure it will become clear eventually."

Weldon and the castle steward did not speak again as they walked. They reached the king's office. The castle steward unlocked the door and pushed the door open. Weldon stepped inside. The place looked like it had not been properly cleaned since Hillel took the throne. Weldon went to the bookshelf. It appeared to have been used more recently, but there was still plenty of dust.

"I should probably let the maids clean in here," the castle steward said.

"It might help," Weldon said, "If we have to come in here to look things up."

Weldon searched through the titles until he found the book he was looking for. It was about where he expected it to be. It felt like a cold draft came through the room. Weldon found himself barely able to keep his teeth from chattering.

"Maybe I will just borrow it for a few days," Weldon said.

"I doubt it will be missed," the castle steward said.

Weldon put it under his arm and left the office. The castle steward followed behind him and closed the door before locking it.

"I should check with the cook," the castle steward said.

"Okay," Weldon said. He took the book and headed back to his office. The clerks were not working, so it was cold and dark. Weldon put the book on his desk before lighting a candle and using it to see to light the fire. He sat there in front of the fire for a few minutes in an attempt to warm up. When he was as cold, Weldon sat down at his desk and started to read.

Hillel stood at the top of the tower of the guardhouse in the border village and looked over the Grackle. The messenger was right in that there were men gathered on the other side of the border. Hillel was sure that it was not Grackle's full army, but it was enough to make his men look like not enough. He probably should have been worried about the upcoming battle; however, he was not. After all, there was more glory when outnumbered.

Someone came up the ladder, and Hillel glanced back to see the town mayor climb up. Hillel turned around to looking over the battle field. The mayor stayed a step behind him.

"This is not a good idea," the mayor said.

"I did not ask for your advice," Hillel said, "Nor do I need it. I know what I am doing."

"Very well, Your Majesty," the mayor said, "The man you introduced as your top officer told me to let you know that everyone is ready."

"Thank you for delivering the message," Hillel said.

The mayor did not say anything else before climbing back down the ladder. Hillel looked out over the battlefield until he was sure the mayor had reached the bottom before climbing down himself. Hillel had spent some of the time after they arrived yesterday, and he had seen the battle field in the light of the setting sun talking strategy with those he decided he could trust among the men who had come with him. He was the one who knew the most about battles and what would work best, so they did not have any suggestions.

This morning they would get the men ready for the attack. Then he would lead the charge. It was all ready. He doubted this would last very long. Then he would have to decide whether to head home or finish the takeover of Grackle. Hillel smiled a little to himself, but reaching the bottom of the ladder, he let the smile disappear. He went to where the men were waiting. Hillel nodded to the man who would lead the second charge before going to the head of the first charge.

"For Proster," Hillel said before starting forward.

People on the other side of the border had noticed what was going on. A similar sized battalion was coming towards them from that side of the border as Hillel led his march. No one drew their weapons yet.

Hillel met the leader of their charge at the border.

"I am Duke Yestin," the man said, "My brother, King Rafe, sent me to demand payment for the lord who was executed."

"I am King Hillel, and I refuse to pay anything as he was a criminal, and I had every right to execute him for his crimes."

"You had no right," Duke Yestin said.

"There is no agreement between the kingdoms to stop me," Hillel said.

"It is customary to return subjects to their king for

punishment," Duke Yestin said, "We do not need an agreement between kingdoms to follow it, just manners."

"Are you accusing me of not having manners?" Hillel asked.

"You have not shown any so far," Duke Yestin answered. Hillel drew his sword and charged at Duke Yestin in anger. Duke Yestin barely managed to get his weapon out and up to defend himself in time. The men behind Hillel took that to mean they should attack as well and started running towards their opponents. Hillel had no problem with that as he felt it was right, but it seemed to surprise the men on the Grackle side who appeared to be waiting for Duke Yestin to give the order. He was not able to do so as Hillel kept attacking him. However, his men realized they needed to defend themselves from the men attacking them.

Hillel kept up his attack just as he did when training with the guards back in the courtyard. Duke Yestin was not able to attack in return as he was busy defending. There was a clash of swords as the two groups of men connected, and the battle started. Duke Yestin was quickly out of breath as he blocked Hillel's sword again and again. Hillel just grinned at that. Duke Yestin did not manage to stop the next swing, and Hillel's blade sliced through Duke Yestin's shirt. It hit the chainmail shirt under it and bounced off. This provided enough time for Duke Yestin to swing his sword at Hillel. Hillel brought his sword up and blocked. He pushed the sword away and attacked.

A battle between one man from each side came up behind Duke Yestin. Hillel was aware of them, but his focus was on Duke Yestin. When Duke Yestin was forced back to back with his man, Hillel thought he might be winning. Suddenly Duke Yestin and the other man spun together. Now Hillel was facing the other man. This one was not breathing heavily despite having been fighting someone else. Duke Yestin and the man were soon no longer back to back. Duke Yestin was moving the fight off, leaving Hillel fighting this new man.

This man was able to push Hillel's blade away several times and attack. Hillel tried to block each attack and was mostly successful. He felt the sword bite into his arm, but it was not deep and did not affect Hillel's ability with his sword. Hillel attacked before the other man could. Hillel realized this man was better trained than Duke Yestin. But Hillel was not going to let that get in the way of his win. The rest of the battle was no longer in Hillel's awareness as his focus had become the man in front of him.

The swords were up. Hillel swung. The man's sword blocked it. Hillel's blade was pushed away. Hillel swung again and hit the other man's sword. The man pushed him away. Hillel swung. The man did not bring his sword up fast enough, and Hillel's sword went through his sleeve. There was blood on the blade as it had cut through the material and the skin. Hillel swung again. The man brought his sword up and blocked. Hillel was pushed back, but he attacked. The man pushed Hillel back and struck before Hillel could bring up his sword. Hillel dodged the blow. He attacked. The man blocked. Hillel attacked. The man blocked. The man swung at Hillel, who brought up his sword to block. Hillel attacked. The man blocked.

Hillel could feel the cut suddenly as if it had decided

it needed his attention now. He pushed those thoughts from his mind as he focused on the fight. The muscles of his arm were starting to hurt. He had never fought for this long and this hard. Sure, he had trained with guards, but this is much different. It was not going to slow him down or stop him, though.

He was so focused on fighting his opponent, Hillel almost missed the second wave of attackers. So, he was not sure what was happening when someone stepped in front of him and blocked the man's next attack. But Hillel realized what was going on in time to stop from hitting one of his men. He backed away from the fight. He made his way through the fighters and back to where it was safer to rest. Occasionally he had to stop his progress to help one of his men in their fight before he could move along again.

Hillel finally reached the safe area. He put his sword away and accepted a drink before taking a seat. There were others there resting. A few were wounded and getting treatment. Hillel had found a seat where he could see the battle field. Both sides were even at the moment. There were two more waves of attackers who could enter battle, but Hillel would not call on them until the second group was tired out enough that they needed a break. He would go back in a few more minutes as soon as he felt he should be on the battle field as much as he could as the leader.

Weldon was already seated at the table in his dining room. In some ways, this room was still strange to him as he had only been using it in the last month since his wedding. Daniella was sitting beside him with Lady Arabella was sitting across the table from them. Her guards were in the other room. The castle steward and the captain of the guard were also sitting with them. They had already greeted each other and had settled in their chairs.

"What did you find about the line for the throne?" Lady Arabella asked.

"There is not one listed," Weldon answered, "There has never been a written down provision for loss of the Proster line. No one ever thought it would ever happen. There is a piece about whether a queen could rule."

"And it says?" Lady Arabella asked.

"That if the king died, the queen or the consort takes over ruling the kingdom," Weldon answered, "So if Hillel dies, you are the ruler and have to name an heir before you die."

"It is good to know that," Lady Arabella said, "Though I am not sure the subjects will accept it."

"They would have to," Weldon said, "It is written into law."

"And you have supporters," the castle steward said, "It is because of your supporters that Hillel was able to execute the lord from Grackle and start his war."

"I am not sure about ruling a kingdom," Lady Arabella said, "I do not think I would do a good job."

"You could announce your heir and then abdicate," the captain of the guard said.

"I suppose that is possible," Lady Arabella said.

"What is on your mind?" Weldon asked, "Aside from not wanting to be ruler."

Lady Arabella was quiet.

"No one can know for as long as possible," Lady Arabella said, "Because if the demon knows he will try and kill me."

"We will do our best to protect you," Weldon said, "If you do not feel safe at the castle, we will find someplace else for you to stay. If there is something else you need, all you have to do is ask."

"There is going to be an heir," Lady Arabella said, "I am pregnant. If Proster has an heir, the demon will try and kill them. I cannot afford to lose this child."

"We cannot afford for you to lose this child either," Weldon said, "I already do a good portion of running the kingdom now, and I can easily take over the rest until the child is of age to take over."

"Would you prefer to stay somewhere else until the child is born?" the captain of the guard asked.

"No, I think it would look much too suspicious if I moved away from the castle," Lady Arabella answered, "I just need to be careful."

"We have been trying to find a weapon to defeat the demon the last few days," Weldon said, "We will keep trying to do that. If we can do that, you and your child will be safe from it."

"Thank you," Lady Arabella said, "As long as the kingdom is running as well."

"It will be," Weldon said.

"I always thought there were specific ways to defeat demons," Danielle said, "And that you had to figure out how to defeat that particular demon."

"It would probably help," the captain of the guard said, "It might help us find it too."

"We will need to figure out how to find it," Weldon said, "I have yet to see it, though I know it is around. I think there was a book from Proster's reign about demons, but I do not know where it is."

"Perhaps in the office," the captain of the guard said.

"The office needs a good cleaning before anyone can search for it," the castle steward said, "Otherwise breathing might be a problem with the amount of dust."

"Why would it not be cleaned regularly like the rest of the castle?" the captain of the guard asked.

"Because Hillel did not want anyone coming in to disturb anything," the castle steward answered, "His orders were specific on that fact."

"Well, he is not there now," the captain of the guard said.

"But he is not dead yet, either," the castle steward said, "He could return from war, despite the odds against it."

"We will just have to do what we can without the book," Weldon said, "At this point, a weapon might do more good."

"How does one figure out what kind of demon it is?" Daniella asked, "Especially if it is never seen."

"We would have figure out some way to see it and then identify it from there," the captain of the guard said.

"Is there anyone who knows what various demons look like?" Daniella asked, "Or even what to do about each type?"

"It would help to have someone who is an expert in demons," the captain of the guard said, "But until recently we have not needed one. The magician who was here might have been useful that direction, but he is long gone."

"I doubt he is likely to be back," Weldon said.

"Could we train our own?" Lady Arabella asked.

"If there is one book and not much else, how are we supposed to train one?" the castle steward asked, "It is not like we can ask for help from a neighbouring kingdom as there are no agreements with any of the close ones."

"There is a resource," Weldon said, "But it is not available unless there is a member of the Proster line living in the castle."

"Well, technically, there is one," the castle steward said.

"But Hillel is not currently there," Weldon said, "So, it is unavailable until either he is back or his child is born, either of which is too long to wait."

"That leaves us searching for something else," Lady Arabella said, "How long will it take to figure out whether there is a weapon out there? Because once we have that, or if we get that, we need to know whether it will work against this demon."

"I have done some questioning," the captain of the guard said, "But so far all the stories from Proster's men are Proster's sword and no other weapons were magical.

"Where did Proster get his sword from?" the castle steward asked.

"According to the story, he disappeared into a portal, and when he came out, he was covered in blood and carrying the sword," the captain of the guard said.

"Like the portal King Driscoll went through and disappeared?" Lady Arabella asked.

"I am not sure," the captain of the guard answered, "It does not sound like it because it was a completely different kingdom than Proster. It was somewhere on the far side of Grackle. Proster, himself, travelled a lot before he invaded this kingdom, and it sounds like there a many portals all over this world."

"Well, if we would lose the person, we should not try to send someone through the closest the portal to look for another magical weapon," Lady Arabella said.

"I am not sure we could find someone at the level of Proster to fight something in a portal even if we could figure out where Proster found his," the captain of the guard said.

"We might as well keep going how we are and hope something comes up," Weldon said, "Because so far everything we have talked about does not seem like it will work."

"Hopefully, we can find some way to defeat the demon and make the kingdom safe from it," Lady Arabella said.

"Hopefully," the castle steward said.

Hillel sat on the ground and leaned against a crate that had once held supplies. The village doctor was wrapping the cut in Hillel's arm that he had just stitched up. The man on the other side of Hillel finished his swig from the bottle of grog before handing it back to Hillel. Hillel took another swig before putting the cap back on the bottle. The pain from his arm was not so bad with the grog.

"How long have we been fighting?" the man next to Hillel asked.

"Far longer than planned," Hillel answered.

"Two months," the doctor answered.

"Really?" Hillel asked, "That long?"

"Yes," the doctor answered.

"It was not supposed to take this long," Hillel said.

"Is it worth it?" the doctor asked.

"Yes," the man next to Hillel answered, "We are

fighting for the queen."

Hillel nodded. The doctor did not look convinced, but he did not say anything more. He finally finished wrapping Hillel's arm and moved on to the man next to him. Hillel tried to make a fist with his hand. He could feel of the muscles in his arm, but his hand made the fist. It was not as tight as he wanted to be. He could still use his sword, and he should get back to the battle field, but he did not move.

He had been on the battle field for hours every day of the past couple of months. His strength and endurance were stronger than when he started, but he was still tired. The glory he had aimed for seemed much further away than when he had started. The being was nowhere around to offer him advice on how to speed things up, and he had thought he did not need it. Now he was wondering if he did need it. He had studied battle strategy before he leaving the castle, and thought he had a good handle on them. Now he was not as sure about the matter.

All the men were getting tired of the battle. But they were still willing to follow their king into battle. The men on the other side also seemed tired, but they were willing to follow the orders of Duke Yestin, who did not lead them into battle. As far as Hillel could see, Duke Yestin stood back and gave orders. The men did listen to him and continued to fight. But both sides were still on the same ground they had started with.

Hillel got to his feet. He felt a little dizzy from the blood loss and the grog. It did not stop him from heading towards the battle field. Hillel was soon in the middle of the fighting. He helped his men as he came along to one who needed it. His arm hurt, but Hillel was not going to let it stop him. He noticed one of his men were down with an enemy standing over him. Hillel ran to them and blocked the sword swing with his sword. It stopped the attack. Hillel pushed the man back away. He attacked the man and again pushed him back.

Someone came and helped Hillel's man off the ground and back to safety. Hillel kept at the attacker. Someone else joined the fight, and they pushed the man back. The man half turned to the other person and managed to hit them. The person staggered back. Hillel swung his sword at the man. The man blocked the swing. Hillel pushed him, and he was moved backward. To keep the fight going, Hillel moved forward with another swing.

The man who had been sitting beside Hillel and had been attended to by the doctor joined Hillel in the fight. The attacker tried to swing in such a way to hit the man hard and knock him away, but the man dodged the attack, and the swing caused the attacker to spin a little. Hillel hit the attacker with his sword and ripped through the attacker's shirt. His sword bounced off the chain shirt underneath, but the hit was enough to send the attacker down to his knees. The man pulled Hillel's sleeve lightly.

Hillel looked back and realized how close to the border he was, which would not have bothered him if it was not for him heading towards a group of enemy men. They looked almost like they were setting up an ambush. Hillel backed up and away from the border. The attacker did not try to follow him back. The enemy men realized they had been spotted, and it was not going to work. They dispersed.

With the pain in his arm and the slight dizziness in

his head, Hillel backed farther away from the border.

"It might be best if you rest for a short while," the man said.

"I think I will," Hillel said. The thoughts in his head that resting would not help him achieve his glory, but physically he knew he needed it. He and the man headed back to the safe area. They sat down and leaned against some crates.

"Thank you," Hillel said.

"You are welcome," the man said.

Hillel felt his eyelids were heavy as was his arm. The grog was muddling his head a little, but this time, Hillel did not try to fight it. His eyes closed, and he slumped over fast asleep.

Weldon was standing out on the balcony. The sun warmed him a little as he was always freezing when he was at the castle. Outside was better, but not by much do to the winter wind still blowing. He had started coming out here because it did not feel like the demon was looking over his shoulder. Now he came out hoping the growth of Arabella's stomach would bring the white wolf back so he could ask for some advice. But she did not.

The door behind him opened. Weldon did not even glance back to see who it was. Instead, the person came to stand beside him, and Weldon looked over to see it was the captain of the guard.

"I have gone through the list of men," the captain of the guard said, "But there are no stories of magical weapons or that anyone beside Proster had one. Maybe you will have better luck with the nobles."

"So far, no," Weldon said, "Any family stories if

there are any, are about Proster's sword and the various ways he gained it."

"I did notice that story changed a bit depending on who was telling it," the captain of the guard said, "But overall they agree he was the one with the magic sword. I started asking if there are any stories about defeating demons. Apparently, it was mostly Proster who fought the demons, and because no one else did it, they did not need weapons used for it."

"I still have half my list of people to talk to," Weldon said, "But if I do not receive different answers, there is not much point in keeping going."

"Does that mean you are going to give up?" the captain of the guard asked.

"Not yet," Weldon answered, "I am still hoping for the one case where the answer is different."

"Has anyone heard from Hillel?" the captain of the guard asked, "I have gotten letters from the men, but they do not provide any useful information about who is winning or what exactly is happening aside from both sides are still fighting."

"Lady Arabella got one letter from him a couple of days ago," Weldon said, "But he did not say much. The battle was still ongoing, and no one had won any ground. They have not lost men, but they are starting to tire out."

"They have been fighting for months," the captain of the guard said, "I am not surprised they are tiring. I am more surprised they have not given up and come home."

"It is somewhat," Weldon said.

"Did Lady Arabella write back?" the captain of the guard asked.

"She had not given me any letters to pass along," Weldon answered, "I am not sure she wants to write to him, aside from telling him to quit being stubborn and come home without whatever glory he has been seeking."

"I do not think she would be wrong to ask him to do such a thing," the captain of the guard said, "I was more wondering if she had informed him about the child."

"I doubt she would do this until the child is born," Weldon said, "Because she would be worried about him poisoning her again."

"But someone might tell him," the captain of the guard said, "Especially since other people have noticed that she is pregnant and they may write to their husbands off at war the good news about the kingdom having an heir."

"If he shows up at the castle demanding to know why she did not tell him about the child, let them hash it out themselves," Weldon said.

"I would not get between them," the captain of the guard said, "But when Hillel went off the war, I expected that within the week we would get a notice that he was dead. Now we are getting word that they are still fighting, and he is still alive, which means, he may survive and return. There is the possibility that we could be charged with treason because we have been operating like he was not going to come back."

"We can explain it away as us trying to keep Lady Arabella safe," Weldon said.

"And you think he would believe that?" the captain of the guard asked.

"She would back us up," Weldon answered, "Given that the demon could be trying to kill us as well as the destruction of the kingdom, I have been less worried about Hillel. I will do what I have to defend my actions if accused of anything by Hillel."

"That does make sense," the captain of the guard said with a nod.

They were quiet as they looked over the courtyard. Weldon could feel the wind. The captain of the guard did not appear to be suffering from the cold in the same way Weldon was. Weldon wondered if the captain of the guard's cloak was warmer than his.

"Have you figured out what is following you are?" the captain of the guard asked.

"No," Weldon answered, "I keep trying to see it, but it seems to be invisible. It is not as quiet as it thinks it is, though. But I have been having trouble identifying exactly where the sound is coming from when I try searching for it. However, it still has not done anything threatening to me."

"Considering how many other things that are trying to harm us, one less thing to defend against works for me," the captain of the guard said, "But it would still be nice to know what it is."

"I will figure it out at some point," Weldon said, "Because I am curious about it."

"As long as nothing changes with it wanting to harm you before you do," the captain of the guard said.

"I hope nothing changes until then either," Weldon said.

They were quiet for several minutes. Weldon watched the activity in the courtyard. It was all the usual stuff. Despite many guards having gone off to fight with Hillel, there were plenty of guards around. Weldon thought about saying something to the captain of the guard, but before he could, a messenger rode in the gate.

"I better go see what this is about," the captain of the guard said. He moved away from the railing, and Weldon heard the door behind him. He did not move. The captain of the guard appeared below moments later. He met the messenger as the man got down from the horse. They spoke for several minutes, but it did not seem urgent as the captain of the guard was not in a hurry once he received the message. Instead, he directed the messenger inside. The messenger must have been sent back to get more supplies for the men who were fighting.

There had been a request for supplies about once a month since they had left, and every time they requested supplies, it was sent to them. No one felt there were any reasons not to send them. Most of the subjects did not know their king was after his own glory and not defending his wife. There was no reason to tell them differently. Weldon sighed at it all. He wondered what life would have been like if his mother had not married Driscoll. Would it have been easier?

The captain of the guard had disappeared, and Weldon realized he had not paid attention to what direction he had gone. They had probably said everything they needed to for the moment anyway. Weldon probably should go inside and get some work done. He had taken over running the kingdom. It had not entirely been by choice or because he had told Lady Arabella he would, so much because no one else was there to take it on.

The door behind him opened. He glanced over, and the captain of the guard was back.

"A request for more supplies?" Weldon asked.

"And an update," the captain of the guard answered.

"Are they winning?" Weldon asked.

"Neither side is," the captain of the guard answered, "No one is gaining ground, no one has more men than the other, and both sides still have their leaders. But the other side has tried to capture Hillel, and only his men saw it in time to save him."

"So, he might not be back after all," Weldon said.

"We will see," the captain of the guard said, "The other side can capture him and not kill him."

"Yeah, but I do not think Proster has the resources to pay the ransom they would want for him," Weldon said.

"People would try," the captain of the guard said.

"They would," Weldon said, "But I am not sure they would succeed."

"I guess we wait and see," the captain of the guard said.

"We will," Weldon said.

The doctor was redoing the bandage on Hillel's arm as he sat there slumped against the crate. For some reason, Hillel could not keep that arm out of reach of other people's swords. At least this time, the last slice would had mostly healed before this new one was added. The doctor had offered Hillel the grog to help with the pain, but he had refused it. Every time he had accepted the grog, Hillel found it muddled his thinking, and he was sure he needed his thoughts to be clear if he was going keep fighting for the day.

The one time he had accepted the grog for the injury to his arm, he had slept for a full day and then had not felt well enough to fight the next day. It had frustrated him, though the men did not seem to be bothered over the fact that he was not fighting beside them. They seemed to appreciate that he did fight with them and not just shouted orders from the back. There were no complaints when he did not fight; he just felt like it was wrong for him to sit out.

The doctor finished his work. He offered the bottle to Hillel again, but Hillel shook his head. The doctor shrugged and then moved on to the next patient. Hillel got to his feet. His head was all right this time. He took his sword in his hand and headed back to the battle field; the battle field that had remained the same size despite the worn ground from so many months of fighting.

Hillel came across two enemies taking on one of Hillel's men. Hillel joined the fight to make it evenly matched. He and his man started to push the enemies back towards the border. Hillel was careful about staying far enough back from the border itself due to several attempts from the enemies in trying to capture him. The man beside him was also careful that Hillel stayed on the right side of the border. But this fight did not seem to be one of those where they were tempting him to come across.

They moved on to other fights. Hillel found someone else who needed help as the man had been knocked to the ground and was still swinging his sword to defend himself. Hillel hit the enemy from behind and caused him to fall to his knees. The man on the ground sliced into the enemy's chest with his sword. The enemy rolled away from both of them. Hillel followed him while his man got to his feet. He did not appear to be injured, just knocked down. He went with Hillel after the enemy.

The enemy barely made it out of the reach of their swords before he tried to stand up. They reached him before he was completely to his feet, so they swung at him as he was still on his knees. He blocked their attacks. They swung at him again. He stopped their swords. He tried to attack back, but he did not have time to free his sword from the block before they attacked again.

Another enemy fighter arrived to help out his friend. Hillel took on this new friend while leaving his man to keep at the enemy on his knees. This enemy moved away from the fight, and Hillel followed as they exchanged blows. This fighter was stronger than any Hillel had fought lately, but he was not going to let it get to him. The fight took most of his attention; however, he kept enough awareness to know where the border was. The fighter did not seem to be pushing him towards the border.

Hillel kept up the fight and tried to stop it from going anywhere. But the fighter would not let the fight stay in one place. They continued to exchange blows as they went. The fight moved to the right and left, but not toward or away from the border. More and more of Hillel's concentration was being taken up by the fight. He was tiring, and his arm was burning. It was now that he was in pain, Hillel wished he had taken the doctor up on a swallow of grog.

Suddenly Hillel could feel someone behind him. He managed to dodge before the sword of the enemy, who had come up behind him, hit its mark. The enemy staggered a bit at the loss of any solid item in front of him. Rather than stay around, this enemy moved along.

Hillel was back facing down the same enemy. He blocked another attack and pushed the enemy back. The enemy only moved one step back before he swung at Hillel, who stopped it.

Hillel could feel another person behind him. Before he could dodge out of the way, the enemy in front of him caught his sword preventing, him from moving very far. But it was not the slice of a blade he felt on his back. It was the slam of a club like object. Hillel felt the air being taken out of his lungs, and he could not get more inside them. He fell to his knees as he tried to avoid his sword as well as the enemy's sword.

One of Hillel's men moved to join the fight, but he was blocked from doing so by an enemy who showed up to fight him off. Hillel tried not to drop his sword as he did not want to lose his weapon; however, the enemy in front of him did not swing his sword at Hillel. The enemy just stood over him. Hillel finally got a gasp of air. He tried to get to his feet so he could defend himself.

There was another blow landed on Hillel's back. This time he lost his grip on his sword and then fell on to his front. This time the trouble with breathing was the dirt in his face. He moved his head to one side. Hillel moved his hand in search of the handle of his sword. Something slammed into his wrists and stopped him from moving his hand. Hillel coughed the dirt out of his mouth.

Hands grabbed him under the arms and pulled him up to his feet. Hillel struggled to get away from the men with their hold on him, but they were stronger than he expected. They moved through the fighters as if they were not solid beings, except their hold on him was very real. He still tried to fight with them, but without success. It was like there was nothing he could do to get free. They dragged him across the border without any of his men able to stop them, and some of his men did try.

The men dragged Hillel to the other side of the fighters on the other side of the border. Duke Yestin stood there with chains to bind him, which was done quickly before Hillel could do anything to help himself.

"Order your men to stop their fighting," Duke Yestin said.

"No," Hillel said.

"We will slaughter them where they stand if you do not do it," Duke Yestin said.

"You will not do that," Hillel said.

"We will," Duke Yestin said, "Shall we let you watch until enough are dead to make you give the order to stop?"

The men holding Hillel up turned him around so that he could see the battle. Duke Yestin gave a signal, and suddenly, the men from Grackle started fighting in such a way to kill. Except that with an increase in severity, the men from Proster also increase their intensity. The slaughter that was supposed to happen did not happen as expected. Hillel could tell because Duke Yestin was making comments showing his unhappiness.

"Maybe you should order your men to stop," Hillel said.

Duke Yestin turned to Hillel and slammed his fist into Hillel's stomach, which caused Hillel to double over. The men holding him let him feel the punch before straightening him up.

"Your men will not win," Duke Yestin said, "You

might as well call them off."

"Never," Hillel said.

"You would let your men die because of your foolishness?" Duke Yestin asked.

"It is no foolishness," Hillel answered, "You threatened my kingdom, and you continue to threaten it. I would never tell my men to stop fighting you."

"That is foolishness," Duke Yestin said.

There was a scream from the battle field that caught everyone's attention. It was one of the men from Grackle. He had a sword from Proster stuck through his stomach. The owner pulled the sword out. The first causality continued to scream as he fell.

"That is not foolishness," Hillel said, "That is slaughtering of your men."

The men from Proster were able to get into positions and prepare for a full charge. The men from Grackle were not expecting anything from the men from Proster, and this sudden organization shocked them. They backed up, those who were still on their feet. Several were already lying across the battle field.

"You will be the next to die," Duke Yestin said, taking out his sword and putting the tip to Hillel's throat.

"Go ahead," Hillel said, "Do you think they will give up and go home after you kill their king? The king they followed into battle? I would suggest you be the one to call off your men."

"Take him to the wagon," Duke Yestin said to the men holding Hillel as he removed his sword from Hillel's throat. The men dragged Hillel away to a wagon and tossed him in the back. One man got into the back with him to prevent him from trying to get away while the other got into the driver's seat. Hillel could barely see over the side of the wagon at his men standing on the battle field.

LUNCH, FINDING THE SHADOW, AND HILLEL'S FATE

Mitchell put the book down. A servant had come into his study to open the windows and replace his drink with some fresh juice. He had not noticed until now. The sunlight was shining onto the floor rather than the wall. This told Mitchell that it was close to lunch time.

He got and put the book back in the box. The next one called to him, but he was having trouble hearing it above the rumble of his stomach. Mitchell left the box of books where they were. He left his study to find out when lunch was.

Mitchell came back into his study with a full stomach. He took the book back out and found his place. Settling into his chair, Mitchell started reading again.

"Did you manage to question more people today?" the castle steward asked.

"No," Weldon answered, "I have spent the morning dealing with kingdom business. But I am running out of people to talk to on the list."

They were sitting at the same table in the dining room, having just finished eating lunch. Aside from a couple of servants cleaning tables, they were alone.

"Have you found anything?" the castle steward asked.

"No," Weldon answered.

"Nothing?" the castle steward asked.

"Nothing," Weldon answered, "Apparently, there was only one magical weapon in the whole group of men who fought so many battles and so many different creatures."

"That leaves us without a weapon to use?" the castle steward asked.

"I have not given up yet," Weldon answered, "But it does not look like much of a chance of finding anything."

"What now?" the castle steward asked.

"I do not know," Weldon answered, "But given that we have had to have someone taste Lady Arabella's food before she can eat, we need to figure something out."

Before the castle steward could respond, the captain of the guard came inside the dining room and came directly to their table. A messenger was following him.

"We just got an update on the battle," the captain of the guard said.

"What happened?" Weldon asked.

"Hillel has been captured," the captain of the guards answered.

"We need to gather the court and Lady Arabella,"

the castle steward said.

"Immediately," Weldon said.

Weldon and the castle steward got to their feet. The captain of the guard and the messenger followed as they went out of the dining room. Outside, the castle steward grabbed every servant who passed and gave orders from the court to be called. Weldon left the castle steward, the captain of the guard, and the messenger to head up to the bedroom of Lady Arabella.

The two guards who stood outside the door came to attention when he came into sight. He knocked on the door. It was a moment before there was any response.

"Yes?" Lady Arabella called out.

"It is Duke Weldon."

Another moment passed, and then the door opened. Lady Arabella stood there. She was dressed but appeared to have been lying down.

"What happened?" Lady Arabella asked.

"We just received word that Hillel was captured," Weldon answered, "The messenger is here to tell us all of it once the court has gathered."

"Let us go and listen to what he has to say," Lady Arabella said as she stepped into the hallway. The guards followed as Lady Arabella and Weldon headed down to the throne room.

When they reached the throne room, Lady Arabella sat down in the chair set up just below the throne. Weldon stood beside it and faced the gathering nobles. Others gathered in the throne room as well, but no one was going to tell them to leave. The messenger was waiting until he was invited to speak. No one said anything until everyone had arrived and had quit shuffling around.

Then Lady Arabella signalled for the messenger to come forward and present his message. He stepped forward and cleared his throat.

"Lord Tabor sent me back here," the messenger said, "Unfortunately, King Hillel was captured during battle and was removed from the area before a rescue could be put into effect. Any attempts to cross the border to gather information has been blocked. However, a missive came from the King of Grackle. It states that King Hillel will be returned if payment is provided along with repayment for the loss of the nobleman King Hillel had executed."

"Was there a number amount attached to the message?" Lady Arabella asked.

"There was," the messenger answered before pulling out the piece of paper and reading the number off. There were gasps of shock through the throne room. Weldon kept his face passive. Lady Arabella did not make any noise, but her eyes widened.

"The kingdom of Proster does not have that kind of money," Lady Arabella said, "Even if we demanded every person in the kingdom, we could not gather that amount, and we would never repay Grackle for the nobleman Hillel had executed."

"What message should I take back to Lord Tabor?" the messenger asked.

"Tell him to send a message to the king of Grackle," Lady Arabella answered, "Proster will not continue the war with Grackle if the king drops all demands. If the king of Grackle does not drop his demands, Proster's army will invade Grackle."

"And what King Hillel?" the messenger asked.

"Tell Lord Tabor to use his best judgement on that

matter," Lady Arabella answered.

"As you say," the messenger said with a bow.

"Any of other questions or comments?" Lady Arabella asked, looking around at those present.

No one spoke up. They looked around to see if anyone else was going to speak, but no one did. Weldon did not feel anything needed saying. The messenger bowed again before leaving the throne room. Slowly everyone else made their way out of the throne room. The guard did not let Lady Arabella leave until it was clear, so she did not get up from her seat.

"Do you think I did the right thing?" Lady Arabella asked Weldon.

"I do," Weldon answered, "There was little else that could have been done about this situation."

"They are not going to give Hillel back," Lady Arabella said.

"No, they will not," Weldon said.

Lady Arabella nodded with a thoughtful look on her face. The guard finally signalled Lady Arabella that she could move. She left the throne room with the guards going along with her.

Weldon stood there for several minutes. He thought about going to his office and deal with the paperwork sitting there. He also thought about finding someplace to sit and think about everything that had happened. He supposed he should talk to the castle steward and the captain of the guard about the events, but he was not sure he was ready for that yet.

A noise caused Weldon to look around. As usual, he did not see anyone, but he could hear them. He looked as carefully as he could. If he could not hear, the person he would think there was no one there. Weldon sighed.

Hillel might not be returning to the castle, but he did leave enough problems without being there himself.

Weldon headed for the door of the throne room. The sound of footsteps followed him. Rather than go to his office, Weldon started to wander the hallways of the castle. He passed plenty of nobles who did not immediately leave after the court was dismissed, but they did not stop him. He passed servants as well, but they went about their work without paying attention to him.

It had been a long time since Weldon had wandered into certain areas of the castle. He reached an area designated at guest rooms, but he was sure they had not been used in years. Outside one room was some furniture, which appeared to be moved out to redo the room. One of the pieces was a dressing room table with a vanity mirror. Weldon stopped and looked in the mirror. He looked the same as he had that morning, though he may have felt older.

Something caught his attention at the corner of his eye. He looked at it without moving his head. It appeared dusty, but he could not see it when he was not looking at it in the mirror. Whatever it was, it was half his height and relatively thin. Then it moved a little closer, and Weldon could hear the same footfalls as he usually heard. Weldon watched in the mirror as the dust covered object moved closer. It did not seem to realize he could see it.

As fast as he could, Weldon reached out and grabbed at the dust covered object. Rather than get a person, Weldon got a handful of fabric and pulled. The object covered in dust was a cloak and under was a boy. Weldon thought he might have seen the boy once or twice but did not who he was. The boy was surprised to have his cloak removed but did not try to run.

"And who would you be?" Weldon asked.

"Raymond," the boy answered, "I am the son of Lord Farren."

"What are you doing following me around?" Weldon asked.

"My father said you were a good man," Raymond answered.

"That does not answer the question," Weldon said.

"He was killed trying to defend against a demon," Raymond said, "Before he died, he told me I needed to get help from a good man to deal with the demon because the demon is going to try and destroy the kingdom."

"I know that there is a demon trying to destroy the kingdom." Weldon said, "How did your father know? And how is someone supposed to help you?"

"I do not know," Raymond answered, "But he knew about the demon because it poisoned him, and that is why he died. I am not sure how anyone is supposed to help."

"Why would the demon kill your father?" Weldon asked, "You said he was Lord Farren?"

"Yes," Raymond answered.

"The name sounds familiar," Weldon said.

"Many people avoided our family because they claim our family is strange," Raymond said.

"Oh, yeah," Weldon said. The name and the face connected in his head. Lord Farren had gained his title by helping Driscoll, and there had been complaints from the rest of the nobles when he did it because Farren was a peasant and a bit strange. There had been rumours about Farren using magic. Weldon looked at the cloak in his hands. The outside was invisible, but the inside was a soft, grey fabric.

"He said you were a good man," Raymond said, "But I should be wary of King Hillel."

"Your father was a smart man," Weldon said, "Why has your mother not missed you while you have been following me around?"

"She is ill, and the servants refuse to let me see her," Raymond answered, "I sneak in late in the evenings because I have not been following you when you go home."

"Was she poisoned too?" Weldon asked.

"No," Raymond answered, "She was ill long before that, but she had got worse briefly shortly after his death. She is back to her usual level of illness now. My father researched it for a long time before he said that my mother could not be cured."

"Did he say what was wrong with her?" Weldon asked.

"Something to do with being part fae," Raymond answered, "But I do not know what that means."

"It usually means it is blood based illness that can be caught by others with similar blood," Weldon said, "The servant are probably keeping you away from your mother to prevent you from catching it."

"I have been with her plenty without getting sick," Raymond said.

"The demon must have felt your father was a danger to its plan to destroy the kingdom," Weldon said.

"If he knew it was there before it poisoned him, he would have killed it," Raymond said.

"Using what?" Weldon asked.

"He has a battle axe, which he said was useful against anything magical," Raymond answered.

"Then it might be a good idea if I speak with your mother," Weldon said.

"You do not need to speak to her," Raymond said, "I can show where to find the battle axe. I am sure she would not mind."

"As an adult, I think it best to talk to your mother first," Weldon said.

"I suppose," Raymond said, "Can I have the cloak back?"

"Are you going to try to run?" Weldon asked.

"No," Raymond answered, "You already caught me."

"Okay," Weldon said as he handed the cloak back. Raymond was careful as he folded it back up. Weldon thought about it and wondered how to find the cloak if it was folded the invisible side out and left somewhere. Such thoughts did not stay around as Raymond led the way through the castle hallways.

At times, Weldon had to give directions as Raymond did not remember which way to get out of the castle. Raymond's family house was much closer to the shopping area than most of the noble houses. The house itself looked normal, but it had a sense of being on its own.

Raymond opened the door, and Weldon followed him inside. No servants greeted them at the door. Raymond led the way up a stair case and into the family end of the house. As they were coming up to a door mid-way along the hallway, it opened, and a servant stepped out. The servant closed the door before turning to Raymond and Weldon.

"Master Raymond, where have you been?" the servant asked, "And who is this?"

"This Duke Weldon," Raymond said, "He needs to talk to Mother about borrowing Father's battle axe."

"I hardly think now is the time," the servant said.

"Is she napping?" Raymond asked.

"No," the servant answered.

"Then it is better to visit now," Raymond said. He went to the door. The servant looked like he wanted to argue but instead stepped back. Weldon followed Raymond into the room. Inside the room were a bed and a door into a dressing room. In the bed was a small woman sitting up in bed. She was very pale, and her eyes were sunken into her face. The lips that were so pale they blended into her face smiled at the sight of her son.

"Mother, I would like to introduce you to Duke Weldon," Raymond said.

She looked up at Weldon.

"Nice to meet you, Duke Weldon," her voice was raspy, "What can I help you with?"

"He needs to borrow Father's battle axe so that he can defeat the demon," Raymond answered, "I told him I could get it for him, but he said he needed to ask your permission."

"Why do you not go get it for him?" Lady Farren asked Raymond. He headed for the door in a hurry to do as he was asked. Weldon did not move.

"Thank you for letting me borrow the battle axe," Weldon said.

"I only ask that you do not leave Raymond out of the matter," Lady Farren said, "He wants to learn how to go against demons and will be despondent if he is cut out of the matter. He wants to lend you the axe because he feels it is a way he can contribute to the fight."

"I do not plan to push him out," Weldon said, "I think I may need more help from him than just the battle axe."

"Do not tell him, but I do not have much time left," Lady Farren said, "He is needed in this world, and I am worried about everyone pushing away causing, him not finding his place."

"I will try to let him help as much as possible," Weldon said, "This kingdom needs someone who knows about demons and what to do about them, so that may be his place."

"My husband started to train him in that direction," Lady Farren said, "But he did not manage to get very far."

"It is more than we have now," Weldon said.

"Thank you," Lady Farren said with a smile.

"Here it is," Raymond said as he came into the room with the battle axe. He was cradling it in his arms and was not moving as fast.

"Good," Lady Farren said, "You go and show Duke Weldon how to use it. Remember, it is your weapon."

"I will," Raymond said.

"Then you better go," Lady Farren said.

"Thank you for your time," Weldon said.

Weldon and Raymond left the room. They closed the door behind them. The servant watched as they went down the hallway. Weldon and Raymond left the house and headed back to the castle.

When Weldon and Raymond arrived in the courtyard, they came across the captain of the guard and the castle steward, who were standing near the gates and talking.

"We were wondering where you went," the castle steward said.

"I figured out who was following me," Weldon said, "And that has led me to a weapon we might be able to use. This is Raymond Farren and his father's battle axe."

"It is a weapon useful against demons," the captain of the guard said, "Just what we have been looking for. We just need to find the demon."

"Is there any reason to wait?" the castle steward asked.

"Aside from the usual business that interrupts us, nothing," the captain of the guard answered, "I will go see if I can find some men to help us go hunting this demon."

The captain of the guard went off. Weldon, the castle steward, and Raymond headed into the castle.

Hillel sat on the stone floor. He had no idea how long he had been there since there were no windows and the guard only delivered one meal. If he had been paying attention, Hillel could probably figure out how many days by how many meals, but he had been so stuck in his head. He had spent the first while trying to figure out if he could escape, but that had been a waste of time. This cell was not meant to be escaped from.

Then Hillel had sat and thought about what got him to this position. He had badly wanted to gain glory for himself. He did not want to just be a note in a history book. His father would be a footnote, except that he had disappeared without a trace and those who returned refused to talk about it.

The only king who was more than a footnote was Proster, and he had gained that through war. Hillel had studied it all and determined that was the route to go. The kingdom of Proster never had an army and instead had used the guards as an army. They had continued the same training as when Proster had trained his men, so if they were needed to fight for the kingdom, they could. Hillel figured they would be a match for Grackle's forces, and he was right. But he had not planned on Grackle fighting dirty.

Maybe if his force had gone full strength right away, it would have turned out differently. His men had worked to keep him out of the hands of the enemy despite his wanting to be on the battle field. Grackle had not been expecting Hillel and his men to be full strength since not all the men were there, and had not fought at full strength to start with. But Grackle had still done the better job of strategizing, or this would have a different ending.

Hillel wondered what they were going to do with him. The kingdom of Proster was thriving, but there was not enough to pay a king's ransom. As much as the people might have supported Hillel's war, they would not support the tax necessary to get even part of a king's ransom, which meant that what happened next would be decided by the king of Grackle, who may choose a life for a life. There some who would not miss Hillel should that be the case, but the kingdom would be in trouble because there was no heir.

It was Hillel's one regret. The one choice he made that he would change if he got to go back and do things over again. There were plenty of crimes he could have pinned on the lord from Grackle, and Hillel had not needed to listen to the being. But he had listened to the being and not thought it out himself. It showed that Hillel was better thinking for himself rather than letting others give him advice.

Weldon sat in the dining room along, with Raymond and the captain of the guard. Supper was over, and the castle steward had left to deal with his duties. The men who had been helping all afternoon had been dismissed before the meal. It had been a long afternoon, and Weldon had wanted to go home too but knew he had volunteered for this problem.

"I do not think we are going to find the demon right now," the captain of the guard said, "Not if we did not find it during our search today. As much as I do not want the demon wandering around now that we have a weapon to defeat it."

"I am going to have to agree with you," Weldon said, "If it is possible, I would say we need more information about the demon and its habits. The problem is figuring those out."

"Yes," the captain of the guard said, "That would be very helpful."

"We will have to try again tomorrow," Weldon said.

"Probably best," the captain of the guard said, "We can leave the battle axe out in the equipment storage as that is out in the courtyard."

"Good idea," Weldon said.

The captain of the guard got up and took the battle axe with him.

"Come on, let us get you home," Weldon said to Raymond.

Raymond nodded as he looked disappointed and

tired.

"We can try again tomorrow," Weldon said as he got to his feet. Raymond followed him. They headed out of the dining room.

"I wanted to be more help," Raymond said, "But I do not know enough about demons to be of real help."

"Of course, you are a real help," Weldon said, "Without you would not be as far into this search as we are."

"Maybe I should spend tomorrow looking through my father's library and seeing what I can learn about demons," Raymond said.

"If that is what you feel is the best way to help us," Weldon said.

"You are not going to tell me what to do?" Raymond asked.

"No, I am not," Weldon answered, "You are going to have to learn to decide what to do for yourself, and if I started telling you, you will not learn how to do it for yourself."

Raymond nodded.

Hillel had his hands and ankles chained along with two guards on each elbow. They seemed to expect him to try to escape. He probably would try had there been an opportunity, but he knew he would not get far in the chains, so the guards were unnecessary. But that was not his decision. Not much was at this point. He could not remember how long it had been since he had been free to make his own decisions. Hillel was almost sure it had been a couple of months since he was captured, but he had not kept count.

The guards pushed Hillel through the doorway they

had been standing outside and into a court room. They entered close to a chair for the accused behind a railing that separated it from the rest of the court room. There was a judge in a chair higher up and behind a desk. To Hillel's right was a large area for the crowd, among which was a man who could only be King Rafe based on how he was dressed and the crown.

Hillel was not allowed to sit immediately, instead, the guards made sure he stayed standing. The trial had already started because the judge started talking as if he had been interrupted briefly. Hillel found the judge's voice was like most and did not hold his attention. Not that Hillel found anything worth his interest. It all seemed to be about the lord he had executed and how the judge found it wrong. There was no person to defend Hillel and his position. They did not seem to feel it was necessary.

The guard nudged Hillel, and he realized the judge had asked him a question. Hillel looked at the judge in confusion.

"Do you plead guilty to murder?" the judge asked.

"I do not plead guilty to murder," Hillel answered, "Because it was not murder, it was justice."

"Enough!" the judge said, "You were only asked what you plead."

"You gave no other choices, and I felt I needed to provide others," Hillel said.

"You are talking out of turn," the judge said, "If you continue, you will be gagged."

Hillel thought about saying more but decided against it. The judge went back to addressing the whole court room. Hillel tried to keep up with him, but his attention kept wandering off. The trial was going on without him.

The guards finally directed Hillel to sit down. It was not a comfortable chair, but better than the stone floor from his cell.

Servants the lord had with him when he visited Proster were brought into the court room and explained their experience. None of them talked about the fact that Hillel had given the lord a chance to leave when they first arrived, or that he gave mercy to the one servant. It was all about the false accusation and the execution. Hillel gave no indication of his thoughts. He felt it best that way.

When the servants had finished their testimonies, the judge took over talking. But he was not talking about the end of the trial and instead talking about taking a break for the night. The guards dragged Hillel to his feet and out the door, so they could take him back to his cell.

Weldon came into the castle and found the captain of the guard and the castle steward standing in the hallway.

"Where is the boy?" the captain of the guard asked.

"He felt that he should spend some time in his father's library looking up demons," Weldon answered.

"Probably a good idea," the captain of the guard said, "Though he was useful yesterday. Does his father have many books on demons?"

"I do not know," Weldon answered, "I know that his father was rumoured to be involved in magic."

"I hope he finds something to do with demons that can help us," the captain of the guard said, "Because we need some way to see the demon so we can defeat it."

"Unfortunately, there is some kingdom business that

needs attending to," the castle steward said.

"I figured there would be," Weldon said, "It will probably be best if I took care of some of that before I help the search."

"Tomorrow is court," the castle steward said, "There have been several complaints about combining the upper and lower court."

"Hillel did that before he went off to war," Weldon said, "That was not a decision I made."

"No, but they figure you would change it back if they complain," the castle steward said.

"You can tell them complaining is useless," Weldon said, "I do not see any reason to change things at this moment."

"I will let them know," the castle steward said.

A messenger entered the castle, and when he saw them, he went over.

"What is it today?" the castle steward asked.

"I come with a message from Lord Tabor," the messenger said.

"You might as well tell us," the captain of the guard said.

The messenger took a letter out of his bag offered it. Weldon took it and opened it. The castle steward read it over his shoulder while the captain of the guard waited.

"Lord Tabor is giving us update," Weldon said, "The fighting has stopped, and the king of Grackle has withdrawn his troops. There was a letter from the king of Grackle saying that as long as we do not try to rescue King Hillel, the king of Grackle is willing to end the war. Information from the capital is that they are putting King Hillel on trial, and if he is found guilty of murder, he will be executed."

"What is Lord Tabor going to do?" the captain of the guard asked.

"He is taking the word we send to do what he thought was best, and he is packing up to bring the men back here," Weldon answered, "He sees no way to rescue King Hillel and also feels it would cause more damage to attempt it."

"That leaves Proster without a king," the castle steward said.

"Arabella can be the ruler until her child is of age to take over," the captain of the guard said.

"She is in no condition to run a kingdom," the castle steward said.

"I will run the day to day things, and she can rule the kingdom," Weldon said, "That is what has been agreed to so far, and I cannot see any reason for that to change until her child can take over."

"We should tell Lady Arabella what has happened," the castle steward said.

"I will go tell her," Weldon said, "And then I will get started on the work for running the kingdom. We will keep searching for the demon, so her child will be safe."

"I have men ready to start the search for the demon," the captain of the guard said, "We will get started, and when the men are back, we should be able to have multiple parties searching the castle."

"I will write up the note that we are expecting Lord Tabor back any time," the castle steward said.

Weldon nodded. The captain of the guard headed back out to the courtyard. Weldon headed upstairs to Lady Arabella's room. The guards were still there, and they did not stop Weldon from knocking.

"Yes?" Lady Arabella's voice came through the door.

"It is Duke Weldon," Weldon answered.

"Come in," Lady Arabella said.

Weldon went inside. Lady Arabella was sitting in the chair with a tray of breakfast in front of her.

"How are you this morning?" Weldon asked.

"I am well," Lady Arabella answered, "How goes the search for the demon?"

"Not well," Weldon answered, "But that is not stopping us from continuing the search."

"Good," Lady Arabella said, "What brings you here so early?"

"We received another message from Lord Tabor," Weldon answered.

"Hillel is not coming back, is he?" Lady Arabella asked.

"He is not," Weldon answered, "The war will not continue if we do not try to help Hillel get away from them and let him stand trial there. They are not likely to let him go."

Lady Arabella nodded.

"We did know it was going to happen," Lady Arabella said, "If he had listened, this would not have happened."

"Yes," Weldon said.

"You will continue running the day to day matters of the kingdom?" Lady Arabella asked.

"Of course," Weldon answered, "I am not going to abandon you or the kingdom."

"Then I think things will be fine," Lady Arabella said, "Thank you for bringing me the news."

"You are welcome," Weldon said, "And you know

that I will help in any way I can."

"I know, and I appreciate it," Lady Arabella said.

Weldon bowed and then left the room. He headed to his office. His clerks were already busy working and did not even look up at him. Weldon sat down at his desk. There was already a large stack of papers waiting for him. Things his clerks could not deal with because he had to.

Weldon started with the top matter. Most things did not break his concentration as he worked, except that his fingers were getting cold. The fire was burning, and it was not as cold outside as it had been, but neither affected him as he sat in his office. He breathed warmth into his hands and kept working.

The trial wore on as Hillel sat there and tried to pay attention, but found his mind trained to wander when others were speaking. It was the third day of the trial and at least two months since he was captured from the battle field. A servant had smuggled a letter into Hillel, and he managed to read it. It was from Lord Tabor, who would have mounted a rescue effort except that it would have caused everything to get worse. The fighting had stopped when Hillel was captured, and it would start again if anything was tried.

Lord Tabor had received word from Queen Arabella that it was up to Lord Tabor to decide whether to attempt a rescue since Lord Tabor was closer to the action. Hillel was relieved that it was Arabella who sent the message rather than Weldon. It meant she was running his kingdom and not Weldon. She would be a good ruler, and Hillel knew that Weldon would not marry her to become king because he was already married. Whoever did win her heart would be the next king, and Hillel hoped it would be someone worth it.

Hillel's thoughts were interrupted by the judge saying something loudly. Looking up, Hillel realized the judge was not talking to him but still addressing the whole court room. It was a recap of what had gone on. Hillel did not understand why they needed to be told as they had all been there for the trial so far. Why would they do this?

"Hillel," the judge said, "It is now your turn to speak. You may defend your actions."

Before Hillel could start speaking, the guards nudged him to stand up. Hillel did and stood at the railing before he started talking.

"I did not murder him," Hillel said, "It was justice. Your diplomate arrived with the idea that there should be a trade agreement between our kingdoms. I told him there had never been one, nor was there likely to be one, but he could stay and present his argument if he wanted. He chose to stay despite what I told him. I gave him time during one of the days in court to give his presentation. He stayed, claiming he was waiting for my response to it. I had no response aside from nothing he had said had changed my mind on the matter.

"He stayed despite no further time at court assigned to him, and I was starting to wonder about that because I would have thought his dismissal was obvious without me having to say it. I slowly became suspicious of him, the longer he stuck around. Then my wife was poisoned. When I investigated, it was found that your lord was in possession of the poison, and his servant had been admitted into her room as the guard thought he was someone else. I had no other choice but to put the lord on trial and then find him guilty.

"I also declared the servant guilty as well, but when it came to his execution, I decided it was not necessary. Just the lord paid for the crimes against my family and my kingdom. Then I sent everyone home so nothing further could happen. It was an execution due to his crime and was not murder at all."

"Is the kingdom of Proster so different that you have no laws on murder?" the judge asked, "Here we have a law saying an eye for an eye, meaning the only crime someone can be executed for it a death."

"It was a death I was executing him for," Hillel said.

"But your wife survived the poisoning," the judge said.

"But the child she was carrying did not," Hillel said, "It is that death for which justice had to be done."

"I see," the judge said. He was quiet for a moment. Hillel did not feel the need to add anything more to what he had already said.

"Anything else?" the judge asked.

"No, I have said everything I needed to say," Hillel answered, "I did what I had to do to serve justice."

"I will add that to my decision," the judge said, "Court dismissed, and I will call it back when I have made my decision."

The guards escorted Hillel out of the court room, where they waited in the smaller room. After a while, Hillel found himself falling asleep on his feet. The guard did not wake him because he did not lean, sway, or fall.

Suddenly Hillel felt the guards poke him to direct him back into the court room. He did as they directed. Everyone was waiting inside the court room. The guards had him stand in front of the railing again.

"Hillel of Proster," the judge said.

He did not wait for a response, and Hillel did not attempt to interrupt.

"You have been found guilty of murder," the judge said, "The laws of Grackle say the punishment is execution. Your form of execution is to be hung until dead, but here we chose to take your head. This will take place next week. A priest will be available for you to repent your sins. Is there a particular saint to which you pray?"

"I do not pray to a saint," Hillel said, "I believe in only one god."

"Then such a priest will be provided," the judge said, "Court is now dismissed as the case is now closed."

The guards removed Hillel from the court room and escorted him back to his cell.

Weldon was almost drifting off to sleep as he struggled to get the paperwork in front of him done. The only thing keeping him from truly slipping into the blackness was the coldness in his fingers. The fire burned in the hearth, but it did not touch him. The three clerks who were now working for him appeared to be warm enough. The weather outside was warming as spring had arrived, and everything was thawing out. Another month and the fire would be too much heat.

There was a knock at the door. Weldon blinked himself away as one of the clerks got up and went to the door.

"Is Duke Weldon here?" the castle steward's voice came from the hallway, "Or is he out again?"

"He is here," the clerk answered. He stepped back to

let the castle steward in, but he did not enter. Weldon got to his feet and went to the door.

"Yes?" Weldon asked.

"It is happening," the castle steward answered.

Weldon was suddenly wide awake, and he hurried after the castle steward. They went through the hallways. They made their way toward Lady Arabella's room.

"I was going to tell the captain of the guards, but he is still searching all the corners of the castle for the demon," the castle steward said.

"I can understand that," Weldon said, "We all wanted the demon caught and gone months ago. With finding the weapon a few weeks ago, we hoped we were close to getting rid of it. Now we really need to do something to protect both Lady Arabella and her child. He will be at supper."

"By then, everyone will have heard the news, hopefully," the castle steward said.

"We will see," Weldon said, "We should wait until everything is confirmed before we make any announcements."

"Very true," the castle steward said.

They reached Lady Arabella's room. The guards were standing outside, and the door was mostly closed.

"How does the situation?" Weldon asked the guards.

"The doctor is in there," the guard answered, "We have only gotten the confirmation that she is in labour and nothing else."

"Then we wait," Weldon said, "This is not something for us to attend."

The castle steward nodded but looked nervous at the idea of waiting. Weldon leaned against the wall opposite the room and let the castle steward pace the hallway. It was pretty quiet in the room, which Weldon thought was a bit strange. However, he would be the first to admit that he did not know anything about pregnant women, labour, and newborns.

After a while, Weldon wondered if the castle steward would have gone off to get some work done rather than pace if Weldon suggested it. Instead, Weldon tried to ignore him. His mind was all over the place and likely as busy as the castle steward was at pacing. He had left a lot of work on his desk, tomorrow was another day of court, Danielle had said something this morning that stayed on Weldon's mind, and the demon still running loose in the castle. There were so many things demanding his attention, but this was where he felt he should be. Daniella had mentioned that she had not heard from Rana is far too long, and she had suggested sending a letter to Rana in hopes of getting a response. If there was no response, Danielle wanted to go visit to see what happened, since Rana had mentioned trouble in the last letter.

There was a noise from the room loud enough they could hear it in the hallway. The castle steward stopped pacing and turned back to the room. It was the crying of a newborn baby. Weldon did not straighten as there was nothing they could do unless Lady Arabella willingly let them inside. The crying quieted down. Another minute went by, and then the doctor stepped out of the room.

"She is asking for privacy for a while longer," the doctor said.

"We can grant her that," Weldon said, "We only ask if there is anything we can announce."

"She says you can tell the kingdom about the birth of her son," the doctor said, "And that the baby's name is Waldemar. However, she requests no one talks about Hillel around Waldemar until he is old enough to understand."

"Then that will be the announcement we make," Weldon said, "Thank you for giving us the message from her. When she is ready, she can send for us."

The doctor nodded. Then he went back inside. Weldon headed back down the stairs with the castle steward following behind him.

"Call the court to hear the announcement," Weldon said.

"Right away," the castle steward said.

Hillel was again chained at his wrists and ankles. There was no escape and no rescue, so he was not sure why they bothered. But they did anyway. The guards today were different from the guards who stood over him during the trial. They gave no expression as they led him from the cell that had been his home for far too long and out to the platform erected in the courtyard. It did not look new.

The guards took him right up to the top of the platform where a man stood. The man had a masked over his head, but there were eye holes so he could see. In front of him was a block stained with rust and in his hand was a huge axe.

"Would you like a blindfold?" the man is the mask asked. The mask muffled his voice, but it was deep.

"No," Hillel answered.

There was a large crowd standing there watching. The king had the best seat to see everything. It was similar to how Hillel had watched the execution of the lord from Grackle. Hillel was pretty sure the judge should have listened more to Hillel's side of things and accepted that Hillel killing the lord had been justice. But apparently, the judge had not accepted any of the story. Now Proster would be without a king because the heir had been killed before he could even be born.

"As determined by the court, Hillel is to be executed for murder," a voice rang out over the courtyard. Hillel could not see the source of the voice from his position. The guards pulled Hillel down, so his head was resting on the stained block. Hillel did not fight them. It would be foolish to try. All he could do was accept his fate as much as he did not want it.

There was another statement from the voice Hillel was not able to see, but he could not make out what was said over his spinning thoughts. The one guard arranged Hillel's collar, so his neck was exposed. Hillel wondered why they had not asked for his final words. There was a noise from nearby that distracted Hillel from his own thoughts briefly. Then Hillel had no thoughts at all.

Weldon stood near Lady Arabella's chair as everyone had gathered in the throne room. They whispered about what this could be about and only quieted when he raised his hand. They fell silent.

"Today, we have a new heir to the throne of Proster," Weldon said.

A cheer came from the crowd. Weldon waited until they had finished.

"Queen Arabella has said her son is Waldemar," Weldon said.

Another cheer went up from the crowd, and this one lasted longer. Some people appeared to get ready to leave, but when Weldon did not move, they stayed still. Weldon did not say anything more until the cheering finished.

"Queen Arabella makes one request of all subjects of the kingdom of Proster," Weldon said, "That request is to not discuss the child's father in hearing range of Waldemar until she feels he is old enough to understand. As announced before, I will help Queen Arabella run the kingdom until the boy is of age to take over."

This resulted in nods from the audience. Weldon then signalled that court was dismissed. The crowd dispersed. Weldon waited until everyone had left before heading to his office. His clerks looked up at him when he entered.

"We have a new prince in the castle," Weldon said.

The clerks smiled and nodded before going back to their work. Weldon sat down at his desk. Instead of started with his work again, Weldon took out a fresh piece of paper. He thought about it for a moment before putting quill to the paper.

My sister, Rana,

I hope you are well as you have not sent much for letters since you moved out to the country estate. Hillel's war has had various complications here. We have been trying to sort everything out since the missive from Grackle arrived to announce Hillel's execution. Arabella gave birth to a healthy baby boy and named him Waldemar. She has forbidden anyone from talking about Hillel in Waldemar's presence until Waldemar is of the age where he understands his father's crimes against the kingdom.

With this news, I was hoping you were still in contact with Luce. He is the only one we could think of who has magical knowledge. If he is available, maybe he can come help us with a slight problem left from Hillel's rein. He would be paid well for any inconvenience coming would cause.

I have taken over running the kingdom. It is a hard job, but I have been doing pretty much the job for a while now, so it was not a big leap. The only difference is that I am now the official leader with the public end of it as well as the running of it. So far, I think I can handle it, but it will be nice when Waldemar is of age to take it over.

Daniella sends greetings. She says you need to write to her more, or she is going to steal a carriage and find you. I think she misses you. Aside from a few complications from Hillel's reign, it is quiet here, and that makes for less exciting things happening.

Anyway, I hope you are well, and I hope to hear from you soon about Luce.

Your brother, Weldon

Weldon let the paper dry as he addressed the envelope. Then he put the letter inside the envelope and sealed it with wax. He set it among the letters to go out. Then Weldon settled in to work.

Weldon was sitting in his office working as there seemed to be more and more collecting every time he went away. He had wanted to help the captain of the guard in the continued search for the demon, but Weldon kept having to put off helping for the work running the kingdom. Raymond had showed up briefly to say that his mother was close to death, and he would not be back for a while. Then Weldon had gone to check on Lady Farren and Raymond to find out that she had died, and Raymond had disappeared. Weldon had wondered what happened, but the servants claimed that Lady Farren's sister came and got Raymond. Weldon did not have time to put towards looking into the matter.

Weldon set his quill down and rubbed his hands together to warm them. As he picked up the quill again, there was a noise at the door. Weldon had given up closing it recently because the nobles would come around demanding things and disturbing everyone's work when they had to visit. Weldon looked over and saw that it was Lady Arabella. She was carrying Waldemar in her arms. He was barely a week old, so he was still sleeping much of the day.

"Can I help you, Lady Arabella?" Weldon asked. He had put down his quill and gotten to his feet.

"I wanted to talk to you for a minute," Lady Arabella said as she came in. One of the clerks gave up his chair, so Lady Arabella could sit down as she talked to Weldon.

"Whatever I can do to help," Weldon said as he sat back down.

"I am worried about whether we can stay at the castle," Lady Arabella said.

"What happened?" Weldon asked.

"There was a servant in my room yesterday afternoon who I had not allowed inside," Lady Arabella answered, "When I stopped the servant from doing anything, he appeared to wake up and then wondered why he was there. I sent him out, and he went without a problem. The guards said they sent away another servant the other day. If this keeps up, they might not be caught in time to prevent something from happening."

"I can offer you some rooms in my house," Weldon said, "Or we can see if someone else we trust can take you in. We are trying to find the demon, but it is not going well."

"What is the problem?" Lady Arabella asked.

"The demon is invisible," Weldon answered, "And we do not know how to find it. How do you see something that is invisible?"

"That is a difficult thing to figure out," Lady Arabella answered, "I never saw the demon, I just heard Hillel talking to it."

"We will figure it out," Weldon said, "In the meantime, we will find a place for you to stay until it is gone from the castle."

"Thank you," Lady Arabella said.

"I told you that I would help you in any way I can," Weldon said.

Before Lady Arabella could answer, there was a knock at the door. Weldon wondered who would be interrupting them. He looked over and saw the castle steward standing there. Weldon realized he should have known that because no one else knocked, they just came in. Lady Arabella turned to look.

"Yes?" Weldon asked.

"Lady Rana is here," the castle steward answered, "Her carriage is in the courtyard."

"Lady Rana is here?" Lady Arabella asked as she got to her feet.

"Yes," the castle steward said with a nod.

Weldon got to his feet and then followed Lady Arabella from the room. The castle steward led the way to the entry way. Rana was entering the main door with one of the guards she took with her following her. In her arms was a bundle similar to Lady Arabella's bundle, except bigger.

"Lady Arabella," Rana said with a smile, "How are you?"

"I am okay," Lady Arabella answered, "What are you doing here?"

"Weldon wrote that you were having some troubles," Rana said, "And I could only think it was demon trouble."

"Why would you think that?" Lady Arabella asked.

"Because when I left, a demon came after me," Rana answered, "We took care of it, and I have been studying everything I can find about demons since then."

"That is exactly the trouble we are having," Lady Arabella said, "Was the demon you took care of invisible?"

"No," Rana answered, "But I am sure I can help you figure out what to do about the demon."

"We need the help," Weldon said. Somehow he was staring at the bundle in her arms.

"I am sorry, I should introduce you," Rana said with a smile, "This is my daughter, Mirian." She moved the blanket enough for Weldon to see the girl. She was at least a month old, probably more.

"She is so sweet," Lady Arabella said.

Weldon found himself not sure what to say. Based on the timeline, Rana had to pregnant before she left, and that likely explained why she was in such a rush to go. But there was a sense of joy at seeing his niece, even if he had not expected her. He offered to take Mirian from Rana, and she handed the sleeping child over.

"How much have you been studying demons?" Weldon asked.

"Luce gave me a crystal so I can talk to him, and he had sent me books to study," Rana answered, "I have them in my bags."

There was noise coming from the far end of the hallway caused everyone to look. The captain of the guard and a group of guardsmen were coming back from their search. The captain of the guard was carrying the battle axe. Since it was close to lunch, Weldon expected the other group they had sent searching would show soon.

The captain of the guard sent his men on to the dining room while he joined the group.

"Hello, Lady Rana," the captain of the guard said with a bow.

"Hello," Rana said, "No trace of the demon."

"No," the captain of the guard answered.

"I am here to help because I have been studying demons over the last while," Rana said, "I am guessing you have searched the whole castle."

"I have," the captain of the guard said, "Multiple times, but there is a difficulty in finding it."

"Lady Arabella said it was invisible," Rana said.

"Have you studied invisible demons?" the captain of the guard asked.

"I have heard of a few, but I have not studied them specifically," Rana answered, "There is always a way to see them, but it is a matter of finding it. Does anyone know what kind of demon it is?"

"No," the captain of the guard answered, "No one had seen it, and we only know it is here because it was giving Hillel advice, and it keeps trying to get rid of Lady Arabella and Waldemar."

"Then we need to get rid of it," Rana said, "Proster cannot afford to lose the queen and prince."

"First lunch and then my and the men will start our search again," the captain of the guard said, "Any help in finding and defeating the demon we would greatly appreciate."

"Lunch would be good before we start," Rana said, "We were barely stopping for meals to get here."

The group went to the dining room and found places to sit to wait for lunch. Mirian woke up, but rather than crying, she looked up at him and smiled. He smiled back. She giggled. He barely noticed when lunch arrived because he was having fun with his niece. It was not until Rana took her daughter back that Weldon noticed the food.

"Thank you for watching her while I ate," Rana said, "It is so nice to eat while the food was warm."

"I did not mind," Weldon said.

"I will need to find someone to watch her while I help you with the demon," Rana said, "She might become an expert in demons later in life, but right now, she is not ready for that."

"You can take her to visit Daniella, and Lady Arabella can go with you," Weldon said.

"I was hoping to visit her anyway," Rana said.

"She will be happy to see you," Weldon said, "Because you have not written in so long she was talking about visiting you. I told her that if you did not respond to this letter, she could go."

"Now she does not have to," Rana said.

"That is good," Weldon said.

"I have no rush to get home," Rana said, "But I cannot stay too long."

"Understandable," Weldon said.

As soon as Weldon finished eating, he escorted Rana and Lady Arabella to his house. Once Daniella had greeted them and agreed to watch Mirian, Weldon and Rana went back to the castle.

They found the captain of the guard and the castle steward were waiting for them in the entryway. There was a group of guards waiting nearby.

"We have a weapon that should be useful against demons," the captain of the guard said, gesturing toward the battle axe.

"A good start," Rana said, "But normal swords do work as well."

"Good to know," the captain of the guard said.

"I have an idea," Weldon said.

"What is it?" the captain of the guard asked.

"Raymond followed me around wearing a cloak of invisibility," Weldon answered, "The way I found him was I saw him in a mirror, and it showed the dust on his cloak that I could not see without the mirror. Maybe if we use a mirror, we could see the demon."

"That is a good idea," Rana said, "Where to find some?"

"There are a couple of mirrors that have recently been taken out of some guest rooms because they are being redecorated," the castle steward answered.

"Take us to where they are stored," the captain of the guard said.

"This way," the castle steward said before heading

off. The captain of the guard followed with some of his men.

"I need to check on something in my office," Weldon said before heading that way. Rana followed him.

"I am sorry that I did not tell you about Mirian," Rana said, "But I knew her birth would cause a scandal."

"It would have," Weldon said, "I am sorry that it would have caused a scandal, but I understand why you did what you did. I am also glad I get to meet her now."

They arrived at Weldon's office and went inside. His clerks were still off at lunch. Weldon felt the coldness as he went over to his desk.

"Are you okay?" Rana asked.

"I am just cold," Weldon answered, "I have just been cold all winter."

"It is not that cold in here," Rana said.

"The fire helps warm it," Weldon said.

Rana did not respond, causing Weldon to look at her. She was going through her handbag for something.

"Do you have any weapons in here?" Rana asked.

"A dagger," Weldon answered.

"Take it out," Rana said.

Weldon did as he told and took the dagger out from the top drawer of his desk. Rana took out a hand mirror and used it to look around the room. She stopped with the mirror turned towards the chair beside the hearth. Weldon looked at the mirror and saw a figure sitting in the chair. It was a humanoid shaped figure covered in dust like the cloak had been. Its head was down as if it was resting.

Weldon took the dagger firmly in his hand and went

towards the figure. He kept checking the mirror to see the figure because otherwise, he could not. Weldon was just about to the figure and ready to stab it when the figure in the mirror jumped up and ran out of the mirror's view. Weldon could feel the whole room warm up.

"Did you not feel the cold?" Weldon asked.

"No, I could not," Rana answered, "But I thought it might be something else since you did not seem as cold before you came in here."

"Lady Arabella came in here this morning to discuss the attempts on Waldemar's life," Weldon said, "I suggested she could stay at my place because that might be safer, but if it heard us, she is not safe there."

"It has not left the castle yet," Rana said, "Let us go search for it."

They headed back to the entry way and found the castle steward, and the captain of the guard were back with three full length mirrors. The captain of the guard saw the dagger in Weldon's hand.

"What happened?" the captain of the guard asked.

"We found the demon in my office," Weldon answered, "But it ran off."

"Everyone spread out," the captain of the guard called out, "Watch mirrors."

"It will look like a dust covered figure," Weldon said.

The men split up in to three groups. Weldon and Rana went with one group, the captain of the guard went with another, and the castle steward with the third group. The group Weldon and Rana went with headed toward the kitchen. Rana kept her hand mirror out but mostly used the larger mirror.

They were getting close to the kitchen when Weldon saw the figure again. It had the back to the wall and was staying out of people's way. It did not seem to realize it could be seen. The men started to go by the figure, and Weldon just about called them back when he realized they were making sure they had it surrounded.

The men were checking the mirror so that their weapons were pointed toward the figure. Before the figure could get between the men, they attacked. The demon blocked the first few swings with its hands. There was a clink as if they were hitting scales. The next few swings were too soon after the other ones, and the demon could not block them as readily. Those swings sliced through something. There were a groan and a screech; but the figure did not collapse to the ground.

The men did not quit in their attacks against the demon. The demon did block a few more swings, but still not all of them. The mirror was no longer necessary as there was black fluid was leaking out of the demon. It was coming out and covering the demon, making it defined more and more of the figure.

Suddenly one of the men swung at the demon, and his sword went through the demon's neck. A head was only visible by the black fluid flowing from its neck as it went across the hallway. The body collapsed on to the floor. The men quit attacking the demon. They wiped their swords clean before putting them away.

"We need to take the body out and burn it," Rana said.

"Might want to keep the head and body separate until they can be burned," Weldon said.

"Why?" Rana asked.

Weldon pointed to the head was. It was no longer across the hallway from the body but was slowly moving back towards the body. One of the men took his sword back out and stabbed it through the head and carried the head off on the blade. Four of the men each took a limb after making sure they have gloves on. They went after the head, but not too close.

Rana followed them to make sure the demon was burned before it got back together again. Weldon was a little slower to go after them. But when they reached the main entryway, he went the direction the captain of the guard had gone with his group. It did not take long to find them as they were going slowly with the mirror.

"Something happened?" the captain of the guard asked.

"We found it, and they are taking the body out to burn it," Weldon answered.

"Excellent," the captain of the guard said, "Men, let us go join them in making sure the demon never bothers us again."

The men headed out to the courtyard with the captain of the guard following. Weldon found the third group and told them the news before going out to the courtyard himself. Two bonfires going; one for the body and the other fire for the head. Both pieces were going up in flames by the time he got there. Everyone was watching to make sure the demon burned. They stayed around those fires until they had burned down, and the demon was ash. When the flames were gone, some guards swept up the ashes and put them in two containers. The men took them off to bury them in separate holes.

Weldon and Rana headed back to his house, to give

the news to Lady Arabella and spent time with Daniella. They had a good evening together. Weldon felt like there was a weight off his shoulders with the demon gone. The kingdom was safe for the moment. Who knew what the future held, but he was not worried about it just yet.

Weldon was out on the balcony enjoying the spring sunshine. The running of the kingdom took a lot of his time, and this was the first time since Rana had left that he had to relax. She had a good visit with Daniella before she left. They were going to write more to each other, or at least they had promised each other they would.

Lady Arabella was comfortable in the castle again. She said there were no more incidents of servants trying to kill Waldemar. She was settling in to raise her son as she felt she should. The castle steward has suggested a nursemaid, but Lady Arabella turned him down. Weldon was sure she did not want anything near her son that would hurt him, and if she raised him, she would know what was close to him.

Weldon sighed. He knew he should get back inside. Straightening up, Weldon started to turn toward the door. He stopped at the sight of the white wolf. The piercing blue eyes staring back. Then Weldon blinked, and the white wolf was gone. It was good to know there was more protection for Waldemar than just Lady Arabella and the guards.

CONCLUSION?

It was an hour later when Mitchell was interrupted. His wife reminded him that Thompson was coming this afternoon, and he had to get some things ready. She left. Mitchell took out the papers, which Thompson would require for his problem. Then Mitchell was going to do some more preparation when the box caught his eye. The books inside called to him.

It would not matter if he read a little bit of the next one before Thompson arrived. He could read the first chapter and then finish his preparations. Mitchell went over to the box and took out the next book. He went over to his chair and opened it to the first page.

ABOUT THE AUTHOR

Heather Mantler is a lover of fairy tales and fables. Her home town is Prince George, British Columbia. Heather is always working on another story as she hopes to finish every story idea that she has ever written down. She was a nominee for the fiction category of the 2012 Prince George Regional Arts and Cultural Awards and short listed for the 2013 John Harris Fiction Awards. Her blog is heathersdomain.wordpress.com. Heather encourages her readers to post reviews on Good Reads and Amazon.